"Don't y[...]

"Canceled it." Drake scanned her from head to toe. She couldn't help noticing the gleam in his eyes. "Ready?"

He looked much too nice in dark slacks and a jacket. The flutter in her stomach didn't coincide with platonic feelings.

"How'd the girlfriend take things?"

"We aren't that tight. Don't worry about it," he said with irritation. Drake hadn't expected her to take his breath away. In the office, she paid no particular attention to her appearance. But now...

He sighed heavily. "I wanted to come with *you* tonight. We're friends, remember?"

She nodded as she gathered up the lacy shawl. The gold against her brown skin made her face sparkle.

Drake continued reminding himself that they were just friends....

Books by Candice Poarch

Kimani Romance

Sweet Southern Comfort
His Tempest
Then Comes Love

Kimani Arabesque

Family Bonds
Loving Delilah
Courage Under Fire
Lighthouse Magic
Bargain of the Heart
The Last Dance
'Tis the Season
"A New Year; A New Beginning"
Shattered Illusions

Tender Escape
Intimate Secrets
A Mother's Touch
"More Than Friends"
The Essence of Love
With This Kiss
Moonlight and Mistletoe
White Lightning

CANDICE POARCH

fell in love with writing stories centered around romance and families many years ago. She feels the quest for love is universal. She portrays a sense of community and mutual support in her novels.

Candice grew up in Stony Creek, Virginia, south of Richmond, but now resides in northern Virginia. This year, Candice and her husband will celebrate their thirtieth wedding anniversary. She is a mother of three, and was a computer systems manager before she made writing her full-time career. She is a graduate of Virginia State University and holds a Bachelor of Science in physics.

Candice loves to hear from readers. Please visit her Web site at www.CandicePoarch.com or write to her at P.O. Box 291, Springfield, VA 22150.

Then Comes Love

CANDICE POARCH

KIMANI
ROMANCE

KIMANI PRESS™

ISBN-13: 978-0-373-86033-3
ISBN-10:   0-373-86033-1

THEN COMES LOVE

www.kimanipress.com

Printed in U.S.A.

Dear Reader,

Thank you for choosing *Then Comes Love,* the second novel in my LOOKING FOR MY FATHER series. Each woman in this series was conceived with an anonymous sperm donor, and at twenty-six each goes in search of her biological father. The first title in this series, *His Tempest* (Kimani Romance, June 2007), was Noelle and Collin's story. *Then Comes Love* is Jasmine's story.

The third book begins in the wilds of Alaska, where the heroine is hiding out. The town's inhabitants regard her as "the mystery woman."

I hope you enjoy the romances of each of the Avery women as they discover their paternal heritage in the opulence of Virginia horse country.

Thank you for so many wonderful letters and e-mails. I love to hear from readers. You may e-mail me by visiting my Web page at www.CandicePoarch.com, or you may write to me at P.O. Box 291, Springfield, VA 22150.

With warm regards,

Candice Poarch

Prologue

The last thing Dr. Drake Whitcomb wanted to do was have this confrontation with Jasmine Brown. Her stepbrother, Steven, should have been the one to talk to her, but the coward had left it in Drake's hands. Of course, the antipathy between Jasmine and Steven was so severe that if she even knew he'd had a hand in it, she wouldn't be there. Since Drake was Steven's frat brother and friend, he wondered why she had agreed to accept the position at the Avery Veterinarian Clinic knowing Drake worked there and must have played

some role in them offering her the position in the
first place.

Drake and Jasmine were both vets. It was Sunday and she'd just moved near Middleburg, Virginia, a few days ago. He hadn't called her, but
simply decided to drive over to her new home.
Fortunately, she was out in the yard talking to the
neighbors. They waved goodbye as Drake drove
into her driveway and parked. She seemed surprised to see him.

"What's up?" Dr. Jasmine Brown asked as she
approached his truck.

"Welcome to Virginia," Drake said, getting out
of his SUV and handing her a vase of flowers.

"Thank you," she said cautiously, clearly
surprised—and suspicious. "Come inside."

"Let's just talk out here. There are a few things
we need to discuss," Drake said. "Especially since
you're scheduled for an appointment at the River
Oaks Thoroughbred Farm tomorrow."

"Okay…" She frowned, puzzled.

"It's about Mr. George Avery, your grandfather."

She sighed. "I imagine Steven has spread it
around to all his friends that I'm the product of artificial insemination, and his son, Mackenzie, was
my donor father," Jasmine said.

"Not quite."

"By the way, do you know how Mackenzie died?" she asked.

"In a car accident last August."

"Well, what did you want to tell me about Mr. Avery?" she asked, avoiding eye contact.

"A month ago he held a large party announcing Noelle Greenwood as his granddaughter. She was also conceived by artificial insemination."

In shock, Jasmine carried a hand to her chest. "Just like me," she said in whispered wonder.

"Yes, like you."

"I've read articles about sperm donors having many offspring, but I never expected..." She seemed to stumble for words and Drake could see the news had thrown her.

"Oh, my gosh," she said suddenly, her wide imploring eyes drilling into his. "Where is she? Does she live here? How old is she? Does she have any siblings? Did she just arrive on his doorstep and tell him? What happened? How long has he known?"

Chuckling, Drake held up a hand. "Hold up. She's twenty-six and she told him quite recently. She only moved here in January. She has one brother, but Mackenzie is not his father. Her brother was conceived naturally a few years after

Noelle was born." Drake gathered a breath. "She spends a lot of time at the farm, so you'll probably run into her.

"As the story goes, her mother grew up next door to Mackenzie. They were childhood friends and her parents were living in L.A. when Mackenzie was in vet school there. When they thought Noelle's father couldn't have children, they asked him to be a donor for them."

"I see."

"And you already know your grandfather inherited the clinic when Mackenzie died last August. River Oaks is one of our largest clients."

Jasmine nodded. Drake settled into the silence as Jasmine absorbed the information.

"Drake, how did I end up with an offer from Avery Vet? I didn't apply. They just offered me the position."

Drake couldn't tell her the truth. He didn't like lying, but Steven had sworn him to secrecy. "When I visited Steven once, I overheard a conversation between you and one of your friends. You told her you wanted to meet your biological father. Mackenzie died soon after I started working here, but he has a family. And I know George Avery will accept you just as he has accepted Noelle."

But Jasmine was shaking her head. "I'm a complete stranger. With Noelle, there's at least a family connection. Mr. Avery knew her parents and grandparents. This isn't the same. He might not accept me as readily."

Steven had told Drake that Jasmine's mother was completely against her moving there and strongly opposed any connection between Jasmine and her donor family. Her own father had abandoned her after he and her mother divorced. Drake wondered if her reluctance to reveal her identity to Mr. Avery had more to do with her own history than with the older man.

He knew Noelle had been reluctant to tell him, too. "It's been a pretty hectic year for him. After Mackenzie died, his nephew tried to pass off an actress as Mackenzie's daughter."

"How awful. The poor man's grieving and his own relative is grabbing for his money." She shook her head. "Does anyone in the office know I'm Mackenzie's daughter?"

"No."

"Please don't tell anyone."

"I don't enjoy keeping things from others, but I'll keep your confidence."

Chapter 1

Performing an ultrasound on a horse might be an indelicate procedure, Dr. Jasmine Brown thought, but after years of vet school she took it in stride. She wore a plastic sleeve covering her completely from her fingertips to her shoulder, and said hand was stuck up the horse's ass, so to speak.

It was a good thing she wasn't squeamish. Of course, by the end of her first year of vet school, all possible squeamishness had been ruthlessly eradicated.

This wasn't just any horse, though. No, indeed.

Maggie Girl was a thoroughbred, the bread and butter of River Oaks Thoroughbred Farm. And horse people loved and took excellent care of their animals. They were patted, groomed and their meals were chosen with precision after years of study based on meticulous scientific research. There was nothing an owner wouldn't do for his horses. From pristine stables that offered better accommodations than many people's homes, to top-of-the-line medical care. The room where Jasmine stood held state-of-the-art equipment from one end to the other.

It was clear the woman standing farther back with men on either side of her hadn't been exposed to this particular procedure very often—if ever. Her face had puckered up an hour ago the moment Jasmine began examining the first horse. She'd examined several horses since, checking to see whether the mares were pregnant. Maggie Girl stood obediently, as if she was accustomed to the procedure.

Chuckling, Burt Taylor, the head trainer, held the animal's reins to steady her. "Better you than me."

"Very funny." Jasmine scowled as she repositioned the probe.

Burt's face was a road map of wrinkles that

deepened when he laughed, which was often, as the man was endowed with a keen sense of humor.

This time of the year, ultrasounds were done practically every day. Jasmine manipulated the instrument until the gray image of the fetus displayed on the monitor. And then she smiled. Everyone smiled. Oh, but there was something special about hearing that little swish of a heartbeat and the slight movement that appeared with it. A large-animal vet, Jasmine specialized in equestrians.

"She's definitely pregnant," Jasmine said. They studied the monitor as workers went about their daily routine, preparing a colt for his maiden race, filling feed tubs and mucking stalls. On a thoroughbred farm there were always a million chores.

This was horse country, near Middleburg, Virginia, and Colin Mayes and George Avery, River Oaks's owners, stood nearby.

Colin, a drop-dead gorgeous male in his late twenties, had an arm slung around the attractive female's shoulder. She had long auburn hair and her complexion was darker than Colin's nutbrown. "You okay?" he asked.

"I'm fine," she mumbled behind her hand.

He chuckled. "How does it feel?" he asked,

squeezing the woman slightly. "Knowing the foal is going to be yours?" He regarded her closely. She finally uncovered her mouth.

"Mine?" Squealing, Noelle Greenwood forgot about the stench and carried both hands to her cheeks before she turned in Colin's arms and kissed him, then looked for confirmation from Mr. Avery. Her grandfather beamed down at her in an indulgent avuncular way.

Jasmine couldn't help it. Her insides burned like acid. She turned away from the scene. It didn't help. Whether she looked or not, it hurt like hell.

"Yes. She's all yours," Mr. Avery concurred.

"Thank you, Colin, Grandpa. I can't believe it! My very own horse." Jasmine faced them in time to see her hug Mr. Avery with such unexpected enthusiasm the older man swayed back before he caught himself. He chuckled out loud and patted her on the back.

Anyone would want him for a grandfather. With his intelligent, aristocratic nature and warm smile even at his age, which had to be mid to late sixties, his form was erect and dashing.

It would be perfectly normal for Jasmine to be envious of Noelle, but she wasn't jealous for the gift of the horse. She'd have her own one day.

Wealthy thoroughbred farms paid enormous vet fees. No, the anger wasn't materially based.

Observing the touching scene between Noelle and Mr. Avery, Jasmine felt a fist squeeze her chest. She closed her eyes briefly in an effort to ease the ache.

In all her life, a man had never loved her. Perhaps that was a bit of an exaggeration, but close. Periodically, memories of her maternal grandfather trotting her around on his shoulders with both of them laughing—emerged. But he'd died a couple of decades ago, so the mental snapshots were sketchy at best.

Jasmine tried to make herself believe she hadn't missed anything. But her heart never, ever listened. Her stomach muscles tightened and anger came swift and sharp, even as she tried to push it away. The horse sidestepped.

"Easy girl," Jasmine said, relaxing her muscles and patting the horse's flank with her free hand. *Take it easy,* she admonished herself. *How would you like some asshole getting tense up your behind?* Examination done, Jasmine extracted her arm and disposed of the glove before she washed up. Pulling her sleeve down, she approached Burt.

"The other four horses are ready to be shipped.

You'll want to wait at least a week and let me do another sonogram before you ship the last two," she told him while she input data into her Black-Berry. The purpose of the ultrasound was to make sure each mare still held her fetus before she was shipped back to her owner.

Burt nodded and Jasmine finished inputting data.

"Call the office and make an appointment for next week," she continued while surreptitiously glancing at Mr. Avery.

"Jasmine," said Colin Mayes as he beckoned her over. "I'd like you to meet my fiancée, Noelle Greenwood. You're going to be seeing a lot of us."

Jasmine approached the couple and extended her hand. "A pleasure to meet you, Noelle." Her stomach was still flip-flopping with an excess of emotions at the unexpected introduction.

"We'd like to welcome you to Virginia by giving a party in your honor Saturday. Please come," Noelle said with an easy smile. "And bring a guest with you."

Jasmine hated parties. People stood around feeling out of place or else indulged in idle chitchat. Waste of time as far as she was concerned. Exactly the reason she worked with animals.

She'd had enough of feeling like a fifth wheel with her own family. Damn, no sense in complaining. She was the new kid on the block, so she had to attend. "Thank you," she said as graciously as she could muster.

Noelle had obviously grown up in the lap of luxury, but there was something genuine about her, and Jasmine felt drawn to her effervescent personality. Besides, this woman was Jasmine's half sister.

She still couldn't believe she had a biological sister—a *half* sister, she reminded herself. This was just too much. Jasmine regarded Noelle closely for similar features. She'd recently discovered George Avery's son, Dr. Mackenzie Avery, had been her mother's sperm donor. Unfortunately, he had died last August. Now she was in Virginia to learn about the family she'd recently discovered. Except they didn't know she was family....

Jasmine wanted to memorize everything to assimilate it all later. Her hair was dark brown in contrast to Noelle's auburn. Jasmine was also a couple of inches taller. They didn't favor at all except maybe the eyes. Noelle had a sweet, pleasant personality. Jasmine certainly didn't.

"I'll send you an invitation informing you of the time," Noelle said.

Jasmine nodded but was still left with a dilemma. She didn't have a date. The only person she knew was Drake Whitcomb and he wasn't a person she wanted to get too close to, even though he'd been friendly enough since she arrived. She was grateful for the information he had provided about her family, and he seemed caring but she didn't trust her stepbrother and therefore, by association, didn't trust Drake.

"Jasmine?" Noelle frowned at her. "Is everything okay?"

Forcing a smile, Jasmine nodded curtly.

"Could you tell the fetus's sex?" Noelle asked hopefully.

"It was in the wrong position. Maybe next time."

"I really don't care which sex it is as long as it's healthy."

There it was again. Another avid horse lover talking about animals the way humans spoke of their babies. Jasmine heard it every day.

"Don't you worry. Maggie Girl is going to produce a fine foal," Mr. Avery said.

Colin smiled. "Especially since she's sired with Diamond Spirit."

"You picked a winner there, son," Mr. Avery said, glancing at his watch. "I have a ton of research to do. Have you had lunch, Jasmine?"

Jasmine glanced at her watch. "No. And I have to get to my next appointment."

"Come up to the house. Leila has lunch ready. She always makes more than enough. Hard working on an empty stomach."

Jasmine's first reaction was to say no, but she stopped herself in time. No sense in cutting off her head to spite her face. She wanted to see the house. She'd also see more of Mr. Avery, her grandfather, and be able to observe her half sister.

Swiftly walking out of the stable, she packed her instruments and stowed them in her SUV before she climbed in. She took a long drink from her bottle of water, then started the motor and followed them to the grand house on the hill.

She'd seen it before—from a distance. Jasmine tried to relax. It was April and flowers had already started to bloom in the yard. An entire garden of azaleas, begonias and God knew what else were bursting with color. And the mountains surrounding them were an explosion of green, even though the temperature still fluctuated considerably from day to night.

She neared the house. It was a picture straight from *Architectural Digest,* Jasmine thought as she parked and exited the truck.

Noelle was waiting for her at the back door.

"Quite a show place," Jasmine said, nodding toward the house.

"I love Grandpa's heated pool best of all," Noelle said. "There's nothing like a nice swim when it's snowing outside and I can't get out to exercise. It's nice having an open invitation to stay here when the spirit moves me."

"You're going to turn into a mermaid," Colin said affectionately, rubbing Noelle's back. He was obviously bowled over by his fiancée.

On the closed-in porch, everyone pulled off their boots. Several pairs were lined up against the wall. After leaving her boots by the door, Jasmine followed them inside.

"Oh, so this is the new doctor," an older woman said, looking up from what she was stirring in a pot. As the aroma hit her nose, Jasmine's mouth watered. "She's as pretty as can be."

Embarrassed, Jasmine stopped in her tracks.

"Leila Nelson, meet Dr. Jasmine Brown." Ms. Nelson might have gray hair splattered through thick black tresses, but her face did not age as quickly as her hair. She was a very pretty woman who looked to be in her late fifties or early sixties. Who could tell these days? Her shoulder-length hair was neatly tucked behind her ears. And she stood no more than five-feet tall.

"Something smells good, Ms. Nelson," Jasmine said.

"You're older than twenty-five, aren't you?" the older woman said, spooning potatoes in a serving dish.

Puzzled, Jasmine nodded. "Yes."

"Then call me Leila. I'm going to see a lot of you around here and I don't plan to go Dr. This and That."

Jasmine smiled, instantly liking the woman.

"Get used to it," Colin said. "She bosses everyone."

"I'm blaming you for the extra five pounds," Noelle said. "I'm going to look like a blimp in my wedding gown."

"I'll still love you, baby, even if I have to roll you down the aisle."

Noelle hit Colin on the arm.

"You needed fattening up, and so does Jasmine." Leila looked Jasmine up and down. "I'll have you healthy in no time."

"You'll scare her before she settles in," George Avery said, coming in the door.

Leila waved a hand. "She made it through vet school, didn't she? She's tough. Bathroom's through there," the older woman said. "You'll find towels in the cabinet. Time to eat." As she talked she narrowed her eyes on Jasmine.

Puzzled, Jasmine started to the powder room when Leila's words stopped her. "You look familiar. Do you have family in the area?"

Only a grandfather and half sister. "No," Jasmine said. "My family lives on the West Coast. I'm from L.A."

"Noelle is from there," Leila said. "Beautiful place. I visited there a few years ago. Anytime you need somebody, give us a call. And I mean that. You're not alone here."

"That goes for all of us," Mr. Avery said.

Deeply touched, Jasmine thanked them and continued to the powder room. Growing up in this family would have been so different from what her life had been. But she wouldn't dwell on it. These people weren't responsible. Her donor father was dead. The man who gave his sperm and didn't give a second thought to his offspring. How could any person do a thing like that? She was a product of him.

Girl, you have to calm down, or else you're going to be a basket case. She had to get through lunch and she couldn't go in there acting as if she was mad at the world. Schooling her emotions was easy. She'd mastered the technique when she was ten.

Jasmine cupped her hands under the water and splashed some on her face. She dried off with a clean towel, giving herself a minute before she joined the others.

The huge dining-room table was laden with food. It was apparent Leila liked to fuss over people. Not used to being fussed over, Jasmine felt uncomfortable.

Through a clogged throat she forced the food down. Conversation volleyed around her and at her. For a moment, she stopped eating and took slow breaths until her stomach stopped turning.

She was finally there, in her grandfather's opulent dining room. Clearly king of his domain, the gentle, soft-spoken man sat at the head of the table, Colin at the other end. Jasmine sat beside Noelle and Leila sat across from them.

Jasmine just didn't understand it. This family had money—plenty of it. Mackenzie Avery had been born in to money. As a veterinarian, he made plenty on his own. Why would he, a man who could offer his offspring everything, become a sperm donor?

"Ouch! You're hurting her!" six-year-old Kelly Kingsley exclaimed. They were in one of the examining rooms in the Avery Veterinary Clinic.

As much as Dr. Drake Whitcomb wanted to wallow in his own problems, he had to get his head back on his job.

"I'm not hurting her, sweetheart. Just examining. Here, feel this." Dr. Whitcomb held the stethoscope to Kelly's hand so that she could see it was harmless. He was getting ready to leave the clinic when they brought the injured collie in. Everyone had left except for the vet tech and office manager.

"Can I keep her?" the little girl asked Drake as if the decision was his and not her mother's.

"No, honey. You already have two dogs and two cats, not to mention the bird and hamster," Marsha Kingsley, the child's mother and Drake's neighbor, responded with a sad smile. The woman clearly indulged her child. "Your daddy will get rid of *us* if we bring one more animal home."

"But what will happen to her?"

"We'll take her to the pound. It's a place for homeless animals."

"It's not fair." The child's face puckered. "What happens if no one comes for her?"

"We'll let the people at the pound decide," Marsha said.

"Mama, can't I keep her? Please? Please?"

Marsha sighed. "I wish we could, but..."

"Tell you what," Drake interjected. "We'll keep her here for a while, at least until she heals."

"What then?" the child wanted to know. "Do you have a dog?"

Drake laughed. "No."

"Dr. Whitcomb spends a lot of time here. He doesn't have time for pets."

"The dog can stay here, too. It's a place for animals, isn't it?"

"You've got a point there," Drake said, and eased the stethoscope in place to listen to the dog's heartbeat. It was a skittish little thing. All nerves. Her coat was smeared with blood, and her hair was dull. She responded as if she'd been a family pet at some point, but someone had recently beaten her with a hard object and she was a bloody mess.

"Ouch," Kelly said again when the animal whimpered.

"Honey, the doctor listens to your heartbeat and it never hurts," Marsha said.

Kelly quieted and Drake tried to keep his focus from straying to the call he'd received an hour ago—a call that literally changed his life.

"Is she going to be all right?" Kelly asked again.

"We'll see," Drake responded, smiling at the child. He was a small-animal vet, and soothing anxious souls was part of the job. "I'm going to take her to the back. While I examine her, I want you to think of a name. We can't call her Dog, can we?"

"Okay. I don't like needles," the child said. "She won't, either." A fist closed around Drake's heart. The child was so cute she'd already stolen his heart. "It's going to hurt." The child's face puckered up as if she was going to cry.

Drake and the vet tech moved the dog to a cart. The tech wheeled her to a back room to take X-rays.

"You can wait out in the reception area, but we're going to be a while. You might want to go home," he said.

"Will you call us and let us know how she did?" Marsha asked. "I'll pay for her care."

"I'll call," he said.

Ponce Rommel, one of the office's large-animal vets, would have suggested he euthanize the animal and be done with it, but that wasn't Drake's way. He gave all his animals the best care he possibly could.

In back, the tech had the X-rays up and ready for him to look at. He viewed them one by one. With at least two to three hours of work ahead of him, he cleared his mind and got started.

The dog was resting in his cage. Drake's customer had left hours ago and he called Marsha to let her know the dog was out of surgery.

He went outside to check on the animals in the barn, the makeshift home he'd arranged for the homeless animals once they'd healed from their injuries. Drake had only been there eleven months, but it was well-known around town that if a sick animal needed a home, Doc Whitcomb was the man to see.

When Drake came back inside, the office manager was still with the vet tech. The office was closed and Drake went in the back to check on the newly-named Hugs. He shook his head. The dog was stuck with the name the child had given her.

"How are you, girl?" Drake sat on the floor in front of the cage and stroked the partially sedated animal. Sad eyes stared into Drake's. It tugged at Drake's heart. He'd planned to leave her at the office. The night tech would keep an eye on her. But her sad eyes touched his again.

She seemed to feel as lonely and as desolate as Drake himself felt.

Who had abandoned her? And why? Drake continued to stroke her fur. Hugs shuddered and settled. What would happen when he left? Hugs would probably feel abandoned again.

He didn't want to be alone tonight. They needed each other. He sighed. He couldn't leave her.

He'd planned to hang around and wait for Jasmine. She was late returning from her appointments. She'd gone out to River Oaks today. He hadn't expected that to happen so soon. Although she'd never admit it, he knew she was apprehensive about her first visit there. He felt as if she was being tossed into the lion's den her first day on the job. The plan was for her to go with Dr. Floyd Parker the first time, but he'd been on another call and couldn't get away.

Drake had no doubt that Jasmine was qualified, but there was a world of history at River Oaks and she was just now coming face-to-face with it.

He was ready for home and needed to get Hugs settled in for the night. "I'm going to get a bed for you, girl. Be back in a sec." He brought himself to his feet in one smooth motion. As soon as he closed the door behind him he heard raised voices.

"What do you mean you're quitting?" the office manager, Jeff Daniels, asked as he sailed out of his tiny office. "You can't quit just like that."

"I sure as hell can," Ponce said.

"We finally got you some relief."

"I'm not having my reputation dragged through the mud with Floyd. I don't know why Mackenzie hired him in the first place. You should have let him go a long time ago."

"Let him go and leave only one vet to handle a practice large enough to keep three working overtime? At least Floyd doesn't harm the animals. He does the routine jobs. And we got you some help, Ponce. We hired Jasmine. You can't just leave the new vet here alone. Think of Mackenzie and all he did for this practice."

"Look, I'll work out my two-week notice, but after that…" Ponce headed to the computer.

"In that two weeks, think about staying. I did a thorough check on Jasmine before we hired her. She'll take all the pressure off you."

"She shouldn't have to. Floyd doesn't carry his load, and you know it. Half the time I have to finish up jobs he starts. I spent half my day doing just that and I'm sick of it. Haven't had a vacation in…I can't remember when."

Desperate Jeff pitched. "With Jasmine here, we'll remedy that."

"But Floyd's still here. Either Jasmine or I will have to do most of the work. Nothing's changed." Ponce sighed. "I don't know. He was Mackenzie's friend and I know George isn't going to fire him. It's not going to do any good for me to stay on longer."

Hands balled in fists, Jeff shoved them into his pockets. "Do you already have someplace to go?"

Ponce shook his head.

Jeff pushed his glasses up on his nose and sighed. "Give us six weeks, please. I'll talk to George."

"When?" Ponce glared as if he didn't believe it.

"Soon, okay? Listen, don't do this to Jasmine. See how things go with her here."

Ponce gave a jerky nod and sat at the computer.

"It's not as if he doesn't offer anything. He's a hell of a salesman. He's brought more business here than we can handle."

"We don't need a salesman. We need full-time vets," Ponce said. "Who will pull their load."

Jeff plucked off his glasses, wiped a weary hand across his face and marched back to his office, closing the door behind him.

This was a long-standing argument between

Floyd and Ponce. Drake had let his feelings be known, but he wasn't going to argue the point over and over. It was Ponce's nature to complain. He always kept the atmosphere tense.

Drake was about to approach Ponce when Jasmine threw open the door and rushed in like a tornado.

"Hi, Ponce," she called out.

Drake remained unseen in back of her.

"How was your first day?" Ponce asked.

"Busy as hell, otherwise okay," she said. "Got a couple of extra calls. Spent more time than I'd intended at the Avery's. Did a few ultrasounds, some injections. Looked at a sick horse. You want a whole list before I put it in the billing system?" she finished as he stared at her.

"Damn it, Floyd was supposed to go there. And he took the tech with him. What the hell has he been doing all day? You should have been off a couple of hours ago."

Jasmine shrugged. "It got assigned to me."

"Need help inserting the notes?"

"Already done on my BlackBerry. Just need to take a quick look to make sure it went over okay."

"Be my guest." Ponce got up and Jasmine slid into the seat, logged in, quickly scanned through her notes and made a couple of notations. With arms crossed, Ponce rocked back on his heels.

"That's it."

"You're kidding?" Ponce leaned over and frowned at the screen.

"I love having my BlackBerry."

"We're going to have to discuss updating things around here, at least if I stay."

Jasmine stopped, glared at him. "If you stay? You're thinking of leaving?"

"We'll see. Don't worry about it. I'm here for now."

Jasmine dragged a hand through her hair. It was windblown, feathery and pretty. Whiskey-colored eyes narrowed with fatigue. Her cheeks had reddened from the wind and her dark blue sweater clung to her pert breasts. There was nothing special about the blue sweater, but what it covered sent Drake into a tailspin.

She got up from the computer and Ponce sat in the vacated chair. Her long legs marched across the floor on a mission. Drake realized he was staring. He fumbled with the door as if he'd just gotten there.

She'd been in just one day, damn it, one day, and already his heart leapt as if he'd galloped a thousand miles. He may not have seen her over the last four years, but he knew her from way back. Didn't help. She had changed so much and now he could get lost in those damnable eyes.

She followed him to the storage room in back of the building.

"I want to talk to you," she said with a curt nod. "Outside."

Drake had expected this. He led the way out back. "What's up?"

"I appreciate your help. But you're Steven's friend and I don't trust him. Never have. Steven has done nothing but play games and made life miserable for me from the moment I met him."

Jasmine paced away, glancing over her shoulder. "This is my career. You mess with me, you'll have a fighting tiger on your hands. And trust me, you don't want that," she said before she marched back into the building, letting the door slam behind her.

She hadn't changed one bit, Drake thought, feeling her boot heels gouging his back. She was still prickly and paranoid as heck. He should have stayed in Vermont. Hell, no. His butt was freezing up north and the pay was only a fraction of what he made here.

Drake opened the door and went to Hugs. Seconds later he felt Jasmine beside him and stiffened, waiting for another shot. He glanced up. She nodded toward the bed. "What's going on?"

"A client brought her in. She's homeless. I'm taking her home."

"Can't the tech watch her?"

"Yeah."

She gazed at him and nodded in understanding. "Need help?"

He waited for lightning to strike. "Sure. I want to limit her movement," Drake said. "So tell me, how did the appointment at River Oaks go?"

For a moment she was silent as they started carrying Hugs's cage to his SUV.

The prickly woman was always on guard. But she was serious about her work. Ponce and Floyd were impressed and it took a lot to impress Ponce. But then, Floyd had watched Jasmine work in Kentucky.

"It went better than I had expected."

"What did you think of Noelle and Mr. Avery?"

"They were both very kind. They've invited me to some party Saturday," Jasmine said, frowning.

"And that's a bad thing?"

She shrugged.

Drake noticed her hands shook slightly.

When animals were out of sorts, a gentle hand and kind words usually soothed them. Her actions were a clear sign of just how much she was rattled, but so was he.

"We've put in a long day," Drake said.

"I have one more stop. A stallion with a hot leg," she said, closing the tailgate. "The trainer thought it should be better by now. Wants me to take a look. See you tomorrow."

"Sure," Drake said, but as he watched her climb into her SUV he wondered why, after the way she'd lit into him, she came back to assist him.

She was some woman, if he could forget her resemblance to Jeckyll and Hyde. Hell of a worker. But personality-wise, she could use some help.

Drake massaged the back of his neck. Knowing that Ponce was considering leaving, he was seriously having second thoughts about bringing her on board. He'd known Floyd didn't carry his weight as a large-animal vet and Ponce was dissatisfied, but he'd been so wrapped up in his own work, he hadn't noticed how bad things had gotten. Floyd often helped Drake with the small-animal portion of the practice, another sore point with Ponce.

Ponce never admitted that Floyd's work had

value. Drake owed his quick success to Floyd.
Floyd was a people person. He might not do the
hard medical work the rest of the vets did, but
with his gregarious personality, people loved him.
He brought new business to the office—business
none of them had to go searching for.

Jeff's car was still in the yard as Drake climbed
into his SUV. He felt sorry for Jeff. The man worried about everything. He had a wife who was
good friends with Mackenzie's ex and she loved
to spend money. No one knew if Mr. Avery was
planning on keeping the practice open. He could
easily sell the practice and all the vets would find
themselves out of work. Jeff certainly couldn't afford to have the practice closed.

Drake glanced toward the barn. He'd wanted to
stop by there before leaving. But not tonight. He
needed to settle Hugs.

Chapter 2

Why was she here? Jasmine had asked herself that very question a million times *before* she came. Now that she was in Virginia—sitting in her SUV in front of her grandfather's vet practice, no less—she continued to ponder.

She could have chosen a dozen different locations. The most sensible option would have been to stay put right in Kentucky thoroughbred country. But she didn't choose sensibly.

The answer was simple when she stopped rationalizing. A thousand questions circled in her mind—questions that had been there since she was fourteen when Steven had told her she was a freak. *It's right here,* he'd said, pointing to a sheet of paper he'd found in her mother's private files. *Your father was a sperm donor. You don't have a real dad. I always knew you were weird.* She'd quickly snatched the paper from Steven and had run to her room to cry behind a locked door. She wouldn't let him see her cry.

After she'd dried her tears she had read the page from top to bottom. Her father was identified with a number and he was listed as an "open donor." It was a couple of years later that she'd discovered that by him being an open donor she had access to his identity when she turned eighteen. On her eighteenth birthday she'd learned that his name was Mackenzie Avery and he lived in Virginia. The next time one of her stepsiblings called her dad a Thing, she'd tossed the name Dr. Mackenzie Avery in their faces.

All the answers led here—at least they had until Mackenzie Avery had died. Right. He was dead. He couldn't answer any of her questions. But his father—her grandfather—was here. Noelle was here. Of course, she hadn't known about Noelle.

And Drake Whitcomb was here, also. She couldn't forget that. Not for one second.

Steven had brought him home from college one year during spring break. Drake was so attractive. Steven and Drake had spent little time at home, since they were always out doing things, but when Drake and Jasmine's paths had crossed he'd always been kind to her. During a family picnic he'd even joked with her while her stepsister and brothers had carried on a conversation among themselves, excluding her, as usual. He was the only friend Steven brought home who treated her decently. And like a starstruck fool she'd fallen for him. But before he'd left, Steven had given her a parting warning. *Don't wrap your little teenage fantasies around Drake, sugar. He eats girls like you for breakfast.*

Since her senior year in high school she'd had a crush on him. What was left over was a lingering case of…what? Love? Like? Whatever it was, it made her blood pressure increase, made her act foolish. She wouldn't name the emotion. And with his six-foot-two stature—a well-built six-two at that, she reminded herself—she could never trust him. Although he could be kind, and was exactly the sort of man she'd be interested in, he was Steven's friend. She didn't trust Steven.

Weary, Jasmine raked her fingers through her already tousled hair and groaned. Why was she doing this? If Mackenzie Avery were alive, he'd probably pat her on the head and tell her *You did very well, honey. Nice to meet you.* He'd signed the papers to release all rights and responsibilities for her even before she was conceived. His obligations were over.

She was a fool. A big fool for longing for something she would never have. She just wanted...her throat clogged...wanted one man, just one man in this godforsaken world to love her and want her. Was that too much to ask for? *You're getting maudlin, Jasmine. Just listen to yourself.* Why couldn't she just let the past go and get on with her life?

That would be too easy. She was cursed to remember everything. Like Drake's midnight eyes, for instance. Penetrating eyes, she thought as she put the gear in Reverse and backed out of the parking space. As if they could ferret out secrets. He was gorgeous, tall and lean.

When he waved with easy grace, as if to say, "I'm patient. You'll come around," Jasmine couldn't help noticing again he was every bit as enticing as he'd been the moment she met him. Subsequent visits hadn't gotten any better. Strong face, short hair and long, thick black eyelashes. In some ways he reminded her of Mr. Avery—at least the gentleness in him if not the features. Who else would take an injured dog home when the vet tech was perfectly capable of caring for her through the night? And that barn out back, a makeshift homeless shelter for animals, was another indication of his generous heart. Floyd had told her he'd modified the building within a month of his arrival.

She couldn't sit there ogling him all day. She accelerated and looking both ways, pulled onto the country road.

She lowered the window to breathe in fresh air. The sun would be setting soon. Some initiation to the job. Her first day was something to write home about.

Nearly ten minutes later, she was bumping down a long dirt path when her cell phone rang. Thinking it was the tech calling her about a client, Jasmine answered without looking at the display.

"I've left a thousand messages for you, young lady," her mother said. "Why haven't you answered any of them?"

Jasmine stifled a sigh. "I've been on the go since daybreak. Anything wrong?" Of course there wasn't. Amanda Brown Pearson was calling her to bug her, as usual.

"Just my weekly call to see how you are."

"Just dandy," Jasmine said.

"I wish you had spent some time here before going to Virginia. They couldn't give you one week off, for heaven's sake? Everyone misses you. We haven't seen you in ages."

Yeah, right. They missed tormenting her. "I'm doing great, Mom. I needed to get settled in. Had to buy furniture and stuff. This place wasn't furnished like the last one."

"Norman and I are coming to D.C. soon. At least we'll see you then."

"What?" *Just what she wanted,* the dynamic duo invading her space, especially since at least one of Norman's children usually tagged along. She'd moved across the country to get away from them.

"The traffic will drive you crazy," Jasmine offered hopefully.

"I live in L.A., honey. I'm used to traffic."

Jasmine ran her hand through her short hair. "If you want to spoil your vacation, who am I to stop you?"

"Exactly. If I want to see you, it looks as if I have to visit you. You've neglected your family. It's time you acted like you were one of us."

"I was never one of you."

"That was your choice."

"Whatever."

There was a long unyielding sigh from her mother. "I absolutely hate that word, Jasmine. You know that."

What else was new?

"I'll call later on in the month to let you know when we'll arrive. And your little brother is graduating from college the end of the summer. We expect you to attend."

Jasmine rolled her eyes. "Just let me know when. I'll fly in for it." He wasn't Jasmine's brother, either, but her stepbrother. They didn't let her forget the difference, and honestly, she never did.

"And we're having a party at the house afterward. You're also expected to attend that. Just because you wouldn't let us give you a graduation party doesn't absolve you from attending the others," her mother declared.

"Mom. I'm not sitting around the house twiddling my thumbs. I have a brand-new job. I can't leave on a whim just to party. I'll get him a gift. I'm sure he'll appreciate that much more than my presence."

"You're part of a family and you're expected to act like any other family member, Jasmine. You've treated everyone shabbily and I'm not putting up with it any longer."

"Your family, Mom, not mine. And they don't run my life or dictate what I do. I'm at the farm. I have a sick animal to tend to. I'll talk to you later."

"Do *not* hang up on me, Jasmine Brown. I'm not finished talking to you."

She'd worked her butt off to get away from home. What made her mother think she wanted to go back there? Jasmine thought as she waved to the guard at the booth outside Three Finger Farms and drove up the path to the stable. Her mother saw only what she wanted to see.

Finally Jasmine heard a sigh. "Jasmine, I know why you're there. You have no right to disturb that man's family."

"I had no right to disturb yours, either."

Her mother sighed again. "I know you hated it from the moment I married Norman. You've pointed it out in a million different ways, but he's tried to be a good father to you, even though you made it impossible."

As usual, it was her fault. She didn't ask her mom to marry a man with a million kids and force them on to her. But that was water under the bridge.

"Mom, I really have to go. I don't live there any

longer. The past doesn't matter." Jasmine finally disconnected and got out of the truck feeling all the energy drain out of her. Conversations with her mother always depleted her.

She might have told her mother the past didn't matter, but she knew better. She'd come to Virginia to come to grips with her past and move on. But who was she fooling? She could have done that in Kentucky.

Except Mr. Avery was here. Her half sister was here. She didn't understand herself. Her donor father was dead. What was it that made meeting his family so important to her? And now that she had, what was she going to do about it?

It was dusk when Jasmine parked in her driveway. As she climbed the stairs to her house three women came out of the house next door, laughing and cheering.

"Hey, Jasmine," Casey Reid called out. She was one of River Oaks's employees and had a relaxed, cheerful personality.

Jasmine waved.

"We're going for a girls' night out. Hit a couple of clubs on U Street in D.C. Want to join us?"

"Long day," she said. "Maybe next time."

"You sure?" They already looked as if they were halfway into a good time.

"I wish I could, but I have to be up before five tomorrow morning. Have fun," Jasmine said knowing very well they'd be out most of the night. She couldn't afford to show up for work half asleep.

"We're going to do plenty of that," one of the women said as they piled into the car. "Take care."

The car started and they drove away. Jasmine watched the women laughing and having a grand old time, and suddenly, the loss hit her. Her stepbrothers and sister would take off on fun ventures like that. She was always on the outside looking in. She'd never belonged with her stepfamily, she thought, as she unlocked her door and entered the foyer.

To the right was the living room, still without furniture. To the left was a family room she'd furnished with two club chairs and matching ottomans. She'd thought to watch TV in there, but so far hadn't had time. Straight ahead were the stairs leading to the two bedrooms and the full bath on the second floor. She'd taken the time to purchase a king bedroom set for the master bedroom, but the guest room remained bare, except for boxes she'd yet to unpack.

Floyd had gotten Colin to pick up her furniture for her on one of the farm's trucks. He and a couple of workers from River Oaks had carted her pieces in. She'd also purchased a table and chairs for the kitchen, but with her mother coming, she had more shopping to do.

Jasmine left her purse in the hall closet and headed upstairs for a shower to rid herself of the horse smell.

She liked her own company, not that she had much time to clear her mind. The vet practice suited her. There was so much to do.

Funny, she didn't often feel lonely. But when she watched the camaraderie between her neighbors, she felt more alone. Suddenly she wanted to share dinner with a friend, chatter nonsense about men the way her silly stepsister often did with her limp-brained friends rather than sit alone in an empty house creaking with age. Maybe she'd invite her neighbors over once she was more settled in.

"Damn it." Drake pounded a fist against the wall. Hugs jumped as Drake slumped in the chair.

"Sorry, Hugs."

The dog settled.

He could not have children. Feeling like someone had blasted him with a stun gun, Drake replayed the phrase in his mind like a scratched record. He couldn't have children.

He was still in shock. He'd had mumps a couple of months ago. His doctor had warned him of the effects of the adult-onset childhood disease. Of course, he'd already known. But he'd wanted to be sure. To see if maybe he'd been spared.

Children weren't something he spent time thinking about. All those plans. Get a good education, build a career, pay off school loans, get married, have children, live happily ever after. The dream. What did it all mean when in an instant such a significant part of it was ripped from you?

So many emotions were jetting around in him. He couldn't focus on just one. Disappointment, inadequacy, such a keen sense of loss, he tried to quiet the anger and fear that was tearing him apart. Although he'd seen the results, he just couldn't wrap his mind around it.

He glanced down at the dog. Hugs had settled on a makeshift bed beside Drake's favorite chair while Drake wallowed in anger and considered what to prepare for dinner. Weary to the bone, he couldn't seem to gather enough energy to move.

He'd already coaxed food into Hugs. And now the animal was peacefully snoozing.

He wanted to think about anything—anything other than the fact that he was incapable of having children.

His cell phone rang, startling both Hugs and him. Drake patted the dog's fur.

Not a call. He moaned. He didn't want to go back out. He picked up the phone from the cocktail table.

"Hey, man. How's Jasmine working out?" It was Steven Pearson, Jasmine's stepbrother. The guy was making a pest out of himself.

"Pretty much the same as yesterday. You've called about her every day. Hell, you didn't care that much when you lived under the same roof. What's with that?"

"Long story, man."

"Huge shift from the man who complained she deliberately ostracized herself from your family."

"Okay. So it wasn't just her. I see things more clearly now that I'm older."

"Didn't look that way when I visited."

Steven sighed. "We weren't the best steps. At least we could have done more to help her fit in."

This was totally different from the story he told in college. "Why didn't you?"

"We were kids, and we were tight. Used to teasing each other. At first we thought we could do the same with her. We didn't understand that she was an only child and wasn't used to that kind of teasing. She took it the wrong way and we kind of thought she was stuck up, so we left her alone—except to torture her. Now I'm seeing we probably tortured her a lot. We were really awful—worse than awful to her."

Drake had a sister and a brother. He could see how forcing three new rambunctious kids like Steven on an only child might be overwhelming. On the other hand, most kids welcomed playmates—someone to chill with and confide in.

"What changed your mind?" Drake asked.

"First, tell me what's going on with her?"

"I really don't like being the mediator." Drake sighed. Hugs lifted her head and Drake patted her. "She met Mr. Avery today and her half sister."

"How did that go?" Steven asked.

"She said it went fine. Noelle invited her to a party next Saturday."

"You're going with her, right?"

Drake grimaced. "Who said I was invited?"

"Well?"

"I got her here. I'm not going to babysit her. She's a grown woman. So don't keep calling me for updates. I have my own problems."

"I don't mean to impose…"

"Yes, you do."

Steven sighed, then said, "I didn't want to get into this, but maybe it would help if you knew the full story. I told you she was the product of a sperm donor, but not about how she found out. When she was about fourteen, I found the sperm-donor papers in a file drawer where Mom and Dad hid their sex books."

"Jeez, spare me."

"Hey. We heard the mattress creak when they thought we were asleep. Anyway, at that time Jasmine didn't know her parents used a sperm donor. I teased her about being a test-tube baby. She didn't take it well, understandably. Look, after her parents divorced, her old man never looked back. He wasn't like our dad. And she never fit in with Dad. You know how he is— unless you invade his turf, his head's in outer space."

"Yeah, I get the picture." Steven hadn't given him the complete details before.

"So, he spent time with us because we were in

his face. Jasmine never bothered him, and he wasn't the kind to reel her in. Wouldn't know how," he said. "Anyway, her dad eventually remarried and had another kid, although her mom claims it's not his. He stayed out of Jasmine's life completely."

What a selfish SOB, Drake thought in anger. He'd welcome a child. And this man just tosses his away like forgotten garbage.

"I just know that she needs help and she'll never get it on her own. Truthfully, she has endured serious emotional abuse. I want to make up for the past, but she won't accept it from me. From any of us. So maybe it would help her to form a relationship with her natural grandfather."

"You're an idiot," Drake muttered. "A little psych 101 and you think you can fix the past?"

"No fair."

"The truth hurts." He should know. "I told her about Noelle, but she isn't ready to tell them."

"Convince her to tell them. Look, you're just the one to make a difference. God. Look at the way you treat stray animals."

"She's not a dog or rabbit, Steve." Drake stopped stroking Hugs. The dog shuddered. The very fact that Hugs was in his house, in his family room, resting by his favorite chair, proved Steven's point. He hated that.

"I'll do what I can," Drake said finally. "But why didn't your parents intervene?"

"They did when they were around, but the worst happened when they were away. Both of them worked long hours."

Drake couldn't help feeling anger at Steven and sympathy for Jasmine.

"You were a real piece of work."

"Don't remind me."

After they hung up, Drake stared at the TV without actually watching, thinking about his few visits to the Pearsons' home. He was older than Jasmine when they met. She in her senior year in high school and he a junior in college. She spent as little time as possible at home, and when her mother forced her to eat dinner with the family or participate in family activities, her anger was such that they all felt the strain. Back then, he'd thought she was just naturally disagreeable. Now, he understood there was a reason for her unfriendly behavior.

He picked up the phone and dialed a restaurant for take-out.

* * *

Drake drove up to Jasmine's house a half-hour later. She wouldn't thank him for invading her space. He should have just chilled out in front of the tube and watched a basketball game with Hugs. But she was new to the area. She'd arrived five days ago and had been going at warp speed since.

He left his car carrying two containers of food. He exhaled and knocked on her door. "Here goes nothing."

She answered in a robe and her short hair was wet and stringy around her face. Even with wet hair she was gorgeous.

"Had dinner?" he asked.

Frowning, she said, "Not yet."

"I have extra," he said, holding up the bag. "Thought you'd like to share."

She moved back so he could enter.

"You can put it in the kitchen. Just give me a minute," she said, closing the door, then rushing up the stairs.

Drake stood in the foyer taking in the atmosphere. There was nothing feminine or inviting about her house. The place was so bare his footsteps echoed through the rooms. There were no pictures on the walls. No colorful throws or pillows to brighten up the place.

Drake slowly went to the kitchen and placed the food on the table. He wondered how the place would look once she'd decorated it.

Pillows were all over his mother's home, along with pretty curtains and feminine knickknacks. He realized he thought of his ideal woman like his mother—warm and soft. He laughed. He was acting like a throwback. Career women didn't turn him off; his mother was certainly one. He grew up with women who were confident and self-sufficient, too, but he was attracted to more feminine women. His mother was strong, no doubt about that. But she had something extra. Something that made his old man's eyes blaze with desire.

So, Drake wondered, what was it about Jasmine that appealed to him? Was it his need to fix her up? He chuckled. As if he could. There wasn't a soft cell in her body. She was all angles and attitude.

A year ago, Steven had asked Drake to check out Dr. Mackenzie. Drake grew up in Fairfax, only an hour's drive from Middleburg. So it was easy to check Mackenzie out when he came home from Vermont on vacation.

He had pretended to apply for the small-animal vet position Mackenzie had advertised. But when Drake went for the interview he found himself impressed with the practice. When Mackenzie offered him the job, Drake discovered that he really wanted to work there, so he accepted.

Now, for no other reason than his friendship with Steven, Drake wanted to help Jasmine fit in with her family. She deserved a break.

Drake heard footsteps descending the stairs and headed to the cabinets to look for dishes. Of course, sharing out of the cartons wouldn't be a bad thing. He gathered plates and utensils and set the table.

He heard her at the doorway, turned around and...he felt the punch of a horse kick in his gut.

Jasmine was dressed in tight jeans and a mauve short-sleeved sweater with a hue that perfectly complemented her complexion. Her rounded breasts were outlined to precision. And the cute V did little to calm his skittering heart. Hell of a lot sexier than the oversized gear she wore for work. He worked to gather his wits.

Drake knew it. He shouldn't have stopped by. He shouldn't have let Steven talk him into taking Jasmine under his wing. Hadn't he gotten in enough trouble behind Steven in college to know better?

"Smells good," she said, dragging Drake back to his senses as she advanced farther into the room. "How is the dog?"

Drake cleared his throat. "Hugs is resting."

"You named the dog Hugs?" Humor shimmered in her eyes. "Do you need one?"

Taken aback, Drake was a little slow in answering. "Are you offering?"

Jasmine cleared her throat. "What was wrong with her?"

"You didn't answer my question," he pressed, though he didn't need the image of her arms wrapped around him. Her breasts pressed against his chest.

"No."

He waited just long enough for the idea of a hug between them—the idea of some sort of physical contact—to hover in her mind the way it was suddenly consuming his thoughts. "My neighbor's daughter named her," he finally said. "Hugs has cracked ribs and several deep contusions. Some idiot used her for target practice."

"Asshole."

"Exactly."

Jasmine smiled, and a dimple appeared in her cheek. He liked that dimple. Wished he could kiss… Whoa.

"Tell me about Ponce," she said, sliding into the chair opposite him. "Why the friction in the office?"

Sitting across from her, he told her about the ongoing battle between Floyd and Ponce.

"Is there any way this can be resolved?" she asked.

"I don't know. Ponce is a chronic complainer. If it weren't Floyd it would be something else. But he is correct in that he is overworked."

"How long has Floyd been here?"

"Mackenzie hired him six months before he hired me."

"I can't afford to have people quit right after I arrive. I can't do the job of three people."

"Don't worry about it right now. I'm sure Jeff is going to come up with a solution."

"Of course I worry. I still have school loans to pay off."

So did Drake, but there wasn't an immediate solution. The seat creaked as Drake settled back into it. He was seeing her in a new light. There were bags under her eyes. He detected fatigue and weariness. And her guard was still up. Having to always guard her back had taken its toll. She didn't know how to relax. He wanted to…

"When is the party?" he asked.

"Next Saturday."

"I'd be happy to…"

She waved a dismissive hand. It grated him that she wouldn't even consider him as an escort. Okay, so maybe he got carried away with his work. And maybe she painted him with the same brush as Steven.

Stubborn woman. He had a date, but he could cancel it—unless it was girls' night out or something. Jasmine would walk through a vat of boiling water before she admitted she needed anyone. The most he could do was just show up on her doorstep at the appropriate time. He was doing this for Steven.

"This party. Is it by any chance for women only?"

"No."

That's what he thought. "So what time is the affair?"

"Don't know," she said, clearly enjoying the food. "Noelle is sending an invitation."

"You are going, aren't you? You're not afraid?"

She glanced up, dark brows pulled together

in annoyance. "Of course I'm going. And why should I be afraid?"

Her back was stiff enough to skate on. She needed to know this family—to at least get it out of her system. He knew he now had to cancel his date. And he'd worked weeks to get the woman to even glance his way….

His cell phone rang and he snatched it out of his pocket. It was the vet tech. An emergency call. He stood before he finished the conversation. "I have to go into the office," he said, closing the phone. "Sorry to cut the meal short."

"Need help?"

"I can handle it. Enjoy your meal."

Jasmine walked him to the door. "Thanks for dinner. And the company."

Drake escaped. He'd never intended to set up his small-animal practice in horse country. The thought struck him again as he made his way to the office. He had been working in Vermont and when he went to check on Dr. Avery for Steven, he was impressed with the idea of heading the small-animal division. Actually his ultimate goal was to move closer to D.C., not Middleburg and he'd planned to do so once he'd saved enough to open his own practice. But last year he'd been charmed by Dr. Mackenzie's mission for the practice's growth.

Now he had to travel just as far as the large-animal vets to get to an emergency, but could only charge a fraction of the cost.

When Drake arrived at the office he gathered the supplies he'd need. Steven had put him in a precarious position. Drake had always been slightly attracted to Jasmine, but her attitude had been the barrier between them. Now that he knew the reason for the attitude…Drake shook his head. God, what a family. He was way out of his league.

Chapter 3

For the party Jasmine dressed in dressy black slacks and a red top—clothing her mother had sent her after despairing that Jasmine had nothing decent in her closet and would never catch a man's eye. Jasmine was never very concerned about what she wore. The horses certainly didn't care. In the mirror she looked at herself critically. She had to admit the two pieces looked nice on her and her mother had saved her a shopping trip. Since Ponce had left a few days earlier for a much-needed vacation, Jasmine had very little spare time.

Jasmine tugged a comb through her short hair, arranging it into shape. There wasn't much to be done there. Usually she didn't bother with makeup, but she applied lipstick and blush—another donation from her mother—and dabbed mascara on her eyelashes to make her eyes appear larger. Stepping back, she realized she didn't look like the usual plain Jasmine. A few minor touches had worked wonders and she approved of the finished product. She picked up the lacy eyelet shawl, also courtesy of her mother. Too dressy. She discarded it.

She'd started up the stairs in search of a jacket when her doorbell rang. Who in the world could that be, she wondered, but only for a second. Drake had shown up with dinner—unannounced—three times in the past week. Did he think she was too skinny? What was up with him? She wasn't too surprised to see him at her door.

"Don't you have a date or something?" she asked. "I heard whispers around the office."

"Canceled it." His gaze scanned her from head to toe. She felt like tugging at her clothes, but the gleam in his eye told her she was looking okay.

"I can get myself to a party."

"Ready?"

She thought he was looking much too nice in dark slacks and jacket. By the last dinner, he'd done a lot to convince her they could be good friends, but even though she tried hard to act like his pal, the flutter in her stomach wasn't friendly.

"So how did the girlfriend take the change of plans?"

"We aren't that tight. Don't worry about it," he said, a little irritated. Drake hadn't expected her to be wearing makeup and looking gorgeous. In the office he was used to seeing her face au naturel, when he saw her at all. She didn't pay attention to her makeup, hair or clothes. Usually her hair looked as if she'd run her hands through it a thousand times. But now...

"Let's go," he muttered curtly.

"If you were going to be cranky you could have gone on your date," Jasmine said in an irritated tone.

Drake blew out a long breath. "How did we get off on the wrong foot? Let's try again. I wanted to come with you tonight. We're friends, remember?"

She nodded. "Just a minute." She gathered up the lacy shawl. "I'm ready." She preceded him out the door, wrapping the shawl around her shoulders. The gold against her brown skin made her face sparkle. The earrings added a feminine touch that tugged at Drake's gut.

He reminded himself they were just friends.

By the time Drake pulled himself together and followed her, she was already seated in the passenger seat. He opened his door and slid in, quickly starting the motor and pulling away from her house.

In the car they were both silent as the miles flew by.

Drake played a Gerald LeVert CD. Jasmine was so tense, Drake patted a hand on her clenched fists, then he took her hand in his, wrapping his around her stiff fingers. Seconds passed before she relaxed her fists.

"It's going to be all right, you know. It's just a party," he said. "They aren't going to tie you up and roast you. They don't even know your true identity."

"I know."

"When are you going to tell them?" he asked quietly as the music filled the car.

"Why should I? My donor father is dead. There's nothing to accomplish by revealing who I am."

"They would want to know."

"They have their lives and I have mine," she said. "I didn't come here to intrude."

For a second, Drake's gaze flickered to hers. "Then why did you come?"

"I've asked myself that same question. I don't know," she finally said after a moment. "The very definition of the sperm-donor program is to give the donor's family anonymity. I don't belong here. It's the way the program was made to be. One happy family gets the child and everyone lives happily ever after."

"Legality can't dictate emotions."

Drake's heart finally began to beat again. The little number she wore had his blood pumping. This was a lot from a woman who usually wore jeans and shapeless tops. He tore his gaze from Jasmine and concentrated on the drive. There was nothing about her that indicated she was coming on to him. She might be dressed for fun, but she was all business.

The music floated around the silence. On a regular date he'd make small talk, but Jasmine wasn't the small-talk type. "So, heard from your family lately?" he asked, before he remembered their estrangement. *Goes to show how shaken he was.* "Forget I asked."

"Good, because I don't want to talk about it."

"I understand."

"My mother and Norman are visiting soon," she said after an uncomfortable silence.

"Oh?"

"They drive me crazy. Mom calls me every week to remind me. How far do I have to go to get away from them?"

"She misses you."

"I doubt it."

"Family's okay," Drake said, but she didn't share his fond memories. "You're going to have kids of your own one day. You'll feel the same about them."

"I'll make sure I marry the father before I have children, or I won't have any. I'm not having a child by a man who doesn't even want them," she said bitterly. "That's for sure."

She had a lifetime of anger to purge. It was apparent in her tone. "What kind of relationship did you have with your father?" Drake asked.

"After my parents split, I can count on one hand the number of times I saw him. I don't think my dad ever really wanted children."

"You know, people start out with good intentions. Life kind of gets in the way. Sometimes when parents get so wrapped up in the mess around them, kids get the shaft. I'm not making excuses and I'm sure your father loves you in his own way."

Jasmine snorted. "I'm too old to delude myself."

Glancing at her, Drake smiled. "What are you? All of twenty-six?"

"I'm an old twenty-six."

"That's right. You were the brain of the family. Graduated at seventeen."

"I wanted to get out of the house as quickly as I could," Jasmine said.

It was just a short drive to the farm, and by the time they arrived at the estate, they had achieved a certain level of comfort.

As she quickly opened her own door and dashed out of the car, once again before Drake could get it, he was again struck by her beauty. It would take a lot to overlook her pain and cynicism and get to the core of the woman. He wondered if she'd ever let anyone see the real Jasmine.

Jasmine had geared herself up for a tedious evening with a group of strangers. Well, that wasn't quite true. Casey would be there, but Jasmine didn't know her neighbor well.

George Avery and Noelle met them at the door. Mr. Avery was very dapper and attractive in a dark jacket and slacks, Noelle more casual in beige slacks and a sculptured aqua top.

Observing the smooth way in which Mr. Avery greeted his guests—a man comfortable in his skin and environment—Jasmine knew he'd passed a few of his genes on to Noelle.

It was when Drake ushered her forward with the pressure of his hand on her elbow, that Jasmine realized he'd touched her at all.

She had been on call that day. It had seemed a horse on nearly every farm needed medical attention. She'd worked from sunup, barely making it home in time to dress for the party. Right now she really wished she could go home, heat up a bowl of soup and go to bed. But she straightened her shoulders and forced a smile on her face to greet her hosts.

"I'm so glad you could come," Noelle said, grabbing both her hands.

"Thanks for the invite," Jasmine muttered. Many people had already arrived. Guests milled around eating snacks and pairing off in conversation.

Noelle hooked her arm through Jasmine's. "Let me introduce you to everyone." She glanced at Drake. "Colin's out back."

Drake regarded Jasmine, and when she nodded, he looked relieved to leave them for male company.

Noelle laughed. "Men. Put them in a tea party and they feel like elephants stumbling around mice."

Jasmine chuckled and her tense shoulders relaxed for the first time in hours as Noelle introduced her around.

In the dining room, the buffet table was set up with finger foods, a cold-cut platter and other hors d'oeuvres. A huge pot of tea was placed near china cups and saucers. It was easier thinking of tea and cakes instead of the fact that she was walking the floors her father walked for many years. That he'd grown up in this house of love as a spoiled only child with both parents.

When they were in a cozy little room with a fireplace and shelves of books, someone captured Noelle's attention and Jasmine had an opportunity to stroll around unattended. She stopped in front of a photo of the man she knew must be Mackenzie. Jasmine flexed her hands around the photo, lifting it for a closer look—and stared into her own whiskey eyes—a masculine image of her nose and mouth. Jasmine's heart pounded. Her palms sweated so much the frame nearly slipped from her fingers. No wonder Leila thought she'd seen Jasmine someplace.

She was the feminine version of her father.

"Hey, girl."

Jasmine jumped, almost dropping the photo. She carefully placed it back on the table next to another one. A man leading a pony with a child on its back. The man was Mackenzie. The girl was surely Noelle. Jasmine forced a smile. "Casey." She desperately needed a moment to pull herself together. Casey was casually dressed in brown slacks and a beige top. Her long hair, usually worn up in a ponytail, hung loosely down her back.

"Sorry I'm late. Thought we'd come together, but I see you got the Doc to bring you. His car looks like it's at your place practically every night. You two an item?"

Gosh, the woman was nosey. "We work together," Jasmine said. She couldn't even have company without somebody noticing.

"So that's what you're doing? Working when he's at your place? Funny, I didn't know you had animals at your place."

"Don't mind Casey," Noelle said.

Casey punched her in the side. "She knows I'm teasing. But take it from me. He's quite the catch. And speaking of catches, when's that brother of yours visiting again, Noelle?"

"I thought you knew. He's spending the summer here working on some geology project," Noelle said.

Casey's eyes blazed. "All summer? Oh…"

"I'm surprised he didn't tell you."

"He did say he had a surprise for me. Don't tell him I already know."

"My lips are sealed."

"How old is your brother?" Jasmine asked.

"Gregory's twenty-one."

"And is he a geology major?"

"Yes, my maternal grandparents left him a cave on their property. He'll probably go exploring there sometime."

"And they left Noelle a summer camp that she's opening this year," Casey said.

"How nice," Jasmine said. "Are you a teacher?"

"No, but my maternal grandparents were. I was a computer-science major."

"Now I know where to go if I have any problems with my computer," Jasmine said with a smile.

"I'm the one."

Jasmine was enjoying herself. Emotions she'd hidden behind a locked gate in her heart found a hole and tumbled through. It was obvious that Noelle had adjusted well to her new status.

She smiled. "I haven't eaten since breakfast. The buffet is calling my name."

"Mine, too. I skipped lunch," Casey said. "Mrs. Leila's food is to die for."

Drake closed the door to the house behind him. Colin was leaning against the truck gazing toward the mountains.

He glanced at Drake. "You got roped into coming, too."

Drake shrugged.

"I was trying to think of a way to escape to the stables."

"Why don't we?" Drake asked, glancing back at the house. "We won't be missed."

"We'll use the excuse of checking on Maggie Girl. Noelle can't complain about that, now, can she?"

Drake chuckled. If ever a man was besotted it was Colin. Drake couldn't see himself being love-sick. He didn't know Colin very well. Met him at the engagement party in March. They'd mentioned the wedding date, but he'd forgotten. Mr. Avery had barbecued a hog and the spread of succulent food had taken every thought out of his head. A single guy got tired of restaurant fare and Drake's own cooking was a far stretch from gourmet cuisine.

"When's the wedding?" Drake asked.

"In a few months. Seems to take forever to plan these things."

"I wouldn't know."

"Trust me. I'm becoming an expert. At least, Noelle is. Talk of gowns, invitations and flower arrangements just goes over my head."

Drake chuckled, feeling a little kick in his stomach. Marriage. Maybe one day he'd marry a woman with a couple of children. But that was in the future. Except Jasmine's pretty face suddenly floated in his vision.

At the stable, some of the men were playing cards in the kitchen.

"Thought you were going to the party," Burt said.

"We were. Too many women chatting away."

"No place for a man, that's for sure."

The men laughed and agreed.

"Once you're hitched, you're not going to be able to get away so easily. You'll really be roped then," one of the men said.

"Oh, stop teasing him."

"May as well let him know the lay of the land."

"Then what are you doing here instead of home with the wife?" Colin said.

"It's Saturday night. She went to D.C. with her sisters."

Burt punched him in the side. "He can't play cards unless the wife goes off with the sister. She's put the pants on you. You haven't played cards in how long?"

"I can play anytime I want. Women don't tell me what to do."

Everybody knew it was all talk. He loved his wife. A few were a little jealous.

"How many grandbabies you got now?"

"Five. Should have another any day now."

"Isn't that something."

"You're going to have a basketball team if they keep going."

"Already got that."

"Colin, when are you going to start?"

Colin wiped the sweat from his brow. "Man, let me get through the wedding first."

"George is going to want some little feet running round that big house. Man don't settle down till he gets some kids. You got to get to work."

Drake felt as if ice was spreading through his

stomach jabbing him with pointed shards. He wished he'd stayed at the house with the women.

"Enough talk about kids. Got food on the counter," Burt said. "Leila sent down some platters for us. Help yourself."

Drake glanced at the countertop for the first time. She'd sent some real sandwiches, not those tiny things just big enough to tease a man.

The party was almost over. When Mr. Avery left Jasmine's side to walk a guest to the car, she was wondering when she could leave discreetly.

"The party was lovely," she said to Noelle. "I had a great time."

"Ready?" Drake asked before Noelle could respond. "Had a great time, Noelle," Drake said, kissing her on the cheek.

"Me, too. We enjoyed having you. See you soon, Jasmine. Maybe we can have lunch or go shopping or something."

"You're talking to a confirmed antishopper here," Drake said.

"We all like to shop," Noelle countered. "I'll call."

Jasmine waved goodbye as Drake led her to the car. He kept giving her strange glances, but she was suddenly too full of emotions to talk.

Chapter 4

"Do you want to talk about it?" Drake asked in the silence of the car.

Jasmine started to speak. She'd spoken too freely with Drake lately. He was Steven's friend, not hers, but his kindness made that important fact easy to forget.

Silence strained between them. "You don't trust me, do you?" he finally asked.

She gauged her response.

"Our conversations stay with us. You don't have to worry about me carrying tales to Steve."

"You're his friend," Jasmine hedged.

"I have many friends. And I keep their confidences." At the stop sign, he paused longer than necessary. His raven eyes pierced her, drilling her with heat until she shifted uneasily in her seat. Reaching over, he lifted her chin with his fingertips. Her skin tingled at his touch. She breathed in deeply, trying to decrease the increasing thumping in her chest. It was pitch dark, with the only illumination coming from the dashboard display. It highlighted his profile and the strong lines of his face. "Do you think you can grow to trust me? Just a little bit?" he teased. His steady gaze bore into her in silent expectation.

Jasmine released a pent-up smile. She wanted to trust him. She'd been tense all evening, before the party and during. Her friends always commented on her serious demeanor, told her she needed to lighten up some. But was this the time? "I don't know."

"I wouldn't hurt you, Jasmine." A car stopped behind them, the headlights shocking them with their intensity. Drake released her and turned right onto a deserted road.

Jasmine pressed a hand to her chest. What was going on here? Could she trust him? Jasmine rubbed her forehead. She simply didn't know.

"It's hard to keep all that stuff bottled inside. Haven't you heard? Stress will make you sick."

All her loneliness and confusion welded together in an upsurge of yearning. She wanted to trust him. "Why are you so concerned about me. Don't start with the false pretenses."

"What I feel isn't false. Have I ever hurt you? Have I given you a reason to distrust me?"

"No, but..."

"What have I done to make you question my motives?"

"You're Steven's friend."

"I'm also your coworker. I'd like to be your friend, too. If you'll let me."

He was smooth, too smooth. "My family's coming to town," she said. "I moved here to get away from them. I'm on my own now. If only my family would leave me alone."

"Was it really that bad growing up?"

"What does it matter? It's over."

"You're talking geography. It's not over in your mind. You still have bad memories about the past. So until you come to terms with it, it will continue to be a problem."

"Who are you, my analyst?"

He chuckled in a deep, rich-timbered voice.

"Dr. Drake Whitcomb at your service… So what did you think of Mr. Avery and Noelle?"

"I spent more time with Noelle and I really enjoyed it. I feel ridiculous for saying this, but I feel the kinship between us. Isn't that silly? She doesn't even know me."

"I don't think it's silly. Did you spend any time with Mr. Avery?"

"Just a few minutes."

"As time passes, you'll have to get to know him better."

She changed the subject. "So what did you and Colin do? You disappeared right after we arrived, until after the party was over."

"We hung out at the bunkhouse, played cards with some of the guys down there. Mrs. Leila fed us real food, not those tiny sandwiches you all nibbled on."

"The sandwiches were delicious. You should have tried them."

"We would have all looked like pigs. We'd have had to eat a million of the things to fill up."

Jasmine laughed. He had the skill of relaxing her and sending heat zinging through her blood at the same time. Nothing had changed. She still liked him. The thought was sobering. This wasn't the direction in which she wished to go.

When they arrived at her home, he got out of the car. She was still thinking about the evening when she realized her door was open. Slowly, Jasmine twisted in the seat. Standing, she wondered if she should even invite him inside or send him on his way. Not to invite him in would be ungracious, even rude. Inviting him inside was tempting fate. She could feel danger coming like an old woman's aching bones predicted rain.

"Would you like a nightcap?" she asked against her better judgment.

"Sure."

What a stupid question. She needed to think this thing through. She was very aware of him as they walked side-by-side to her door. With her mind wrapped around Drake's nearness she was incapable of rational thought. Her mouth had already gotten her into trouble. "I only have wine."

"Sounds good." Drake hadn't expected her to invite him in or to remain seated in the car long enough for him to open the door for her. She must be really out of it. Which made him feel like a heel because all he really wanted to do was kiss her. Her subtle perfume whirled around him, enticing him to the edge of his sanity. She looked like a dream. Why was she so appealing to him? She was so not his type.

Jasmine took the keys out of her purse and fumbled with them. Then unlocked the door.

Drake shook his head. He should get in his car and drive away before it was too late to save himself.

Inside, Jasmine poured wine as efficiently as she did everything else. For her, the electricity in the car may as well have never happened. Just once, he wanted to rock that efficient barrier.

She handed him the glass. He sat in one of the club chairs, stretching out his long legs, wishing for a sofa. She eased on the edge of the chair across from him. He was making her nervous. Maybe he should leave. Neither of them was ready for a relationship deeper than friendship. That was, if he could get her to trust him that much.

Drake finished his drink and stood. Happily, Jasmine stood, too.

"Early day tomorrow," he said.

"Yeah, me, too."

At the door, they stood close and the aroma of her perfume filled his senses once again. She was nearly touching him. His gaze roved lazily over her. He had only to bend a little to taste her soft lips. He never realized before how soft they looked. Most of the lipstick had rubbed off.

A force he was powerless to resist pulled him to her. Drake slid his fingers through her hair and slowly trailed down to her soft cheek and her neck to gently grip her by the shoulders. Drawing her closer, he kissed her lips.

Even though he gave her plenty of time to resist, he couldn't have stopped if his life depended on it. She opened her mouth beneath his teasing lips. Waves of desire rushed through him and he pulled her tightly against him. His lips touched hers again. His whole being was filled with her essence. It was an incredible kiss, a potent kiss. And it was sweet, too. So sweet, he wanted to lose himself in the softness.

He expected her to jerk back, but her hands eased beneath his jacket moving slowly on his waist. Their tongues dueled to a magic all their own. He sighed with regret when she stirred, pulling back. Drake's first impulse was to drag her into his arms, but he didn't touch her. If he did...

He released a long pent-up breath, trying to ease the ache in his loins.

Jasmine looked away from those amazing eyes. They amplified all the heat she'd seen in them in

the last two weeks. Had it only been that long
since she arrived? She felt as if she'd known him a
lifetime and that she'd wanted him at least that
long.

She trained her eyes on his hands. If she didn't
look away she'd do something stupid like drag
him into *her* arms this time.

She swiped her tongue over her lips. Drake
wanted to outline her lips with his own tongue.
Taste the sweet nectar of her again. Who would
have guessed such a prickly woman was so soft
and tender underneath?

"I thought we were friends," she said in a husky
tone, so unlike her natural voice.

Drake cleared his throat. "Yes, well, I'm not
feeling very friendly right now."

"Drake…"

"I know. I know. I won't take this where you
don't want to go. Even if it kills me."

"I don't want to go there."

He smoothed her hair back from her face.
"That's not what your kiss was telling me," he said
quietly.

"Yeah, well, I lost my mind for a second there."

"Hmm." He wouldn't pressure her—not now.

They worked in the same office. And there was too much baggage to sort out there.

He kissed her on the cheek and slid his lips an inch over and kissed her again, deeper this time. He swept his tongue into her mouth. It was a kiss that promised her the likes of nothing she'd clearly felt before, and then she moved out of his reach.

He cleared his throat. "I'll see you Monday."

She only nodded.

The hardest thing he ever did was walk through that door and down the steps. He heard it quickly close behind him. Drake stood there a moment, hearing her footsteps in the family room. He strolled to his car, started the motor and sat staring at the house. The downstairs lights went out. Seconds later the bedroom light came on.

He moaned and drove off. Before he could get even halfway home, Drake's cell phone rang. He could only hope it was Jasmine, but knew it wasn't. He glanced at the number. It was Steven. He ignored the call. He wasn't ready to talk to Steven yet. And he wasn't going to carry stories back and forth between Jasmine and him.

Steven was his friend, but he wouldn't betray Jasmine. She was as far from his ideal woman as she could possibly be. Yet there was something between them he just couldn't ignore any longer.

Drake visited his parents in Vienna the next morning. Knowing his parents would drag him to church, he'd worn his suit, leaving a change of clothing in the car. He needed this opportunity to give him a chance to clear his mind.

Usually he listened to the sermon, but his mind kept straying from the message. Jasmine's anguished face disturbed his concentration. Everything about her made him uneasy. Before he knew it, the Benediction was over and the congregation started pouring out of the church.

It gave him an opportunity to see a few old high-school friends he hadn't seen in years. One was an assistant pastor. They talked for ten minutes before Drake left, feeling a lot better than he had before he'd come.

Early that morning, his mother had gotten up to prepare a feast. The food was all done by the time they all piled into the house, the aroma enticing them to the kitchen. Drake started taking tops off the pots.

"Food will be on the table soon," his mother said. "Get out of my kitchen."

His sister and brother were there. So were his uncle and aunt, and their daughter with her husband and toddler. Drake sighed. Less food for him to take home as leftovers.

"It's certainly nice to have my family home for a change," his mother said as she sat at the table. "I don't see you enough."

There was very little talk as they were gobbling fried chicken, barbecue meatloaf and macaroni and cheese, collard greens and candied yams.

"Ma'am, this food sure is good," his cousin's husband said. "Don't get food like this every day."

His cousin gave him the look that said it'd be a cold day in hell before he got a meal like that again. Drake shook his head. He should know better, but he was young. Their little girl banged the spoon on the high chair situated between the couple.

"Son," his uncle said. "I don't get too many meals like this, either. Drake, you need to know this, because we expect you to be the first to marry. Better live close to home or else learn to cook. Women don't cook the way they used to. I've had my share of boxed dinners. Boxed macaroni and cheese isn't the same."

"You're all talk," his aunt said. "We work, too. What do you think we are, machines? We have to work all week and all weekend. Who's going to stand in a kitchen for hours to cook? You men are too spoiled. You expect everything out of a woman. Better stop watching those TV programs and come back to reality."

"I'm eating a good meal now, aren't I?" his uncle rebutted.

"I'm so glad you've moved closer to home, Drake, but I don't see very much of you," his mother injected to end what was quickly escalating into an argument.

"Work doesn't leave very much free time."

"Maybe your office needs more vets," his mother added.

Drake shrugged. "Maybe."

"Didn't you say the sister of a friend of yours was coming?"

"She's here, but she works mostly with horses. Most of her work is in the field."

"Is she a nice young lady?" his mother wanted to know.

"Yes, Mom, she is. And there's nothing between us." At least not yet, Drake thought.

"You're not getting any younger," his sister, Gail, said. "Don't I see some gray in your hair?"

"Is that dye in yours?" Drake responded. "I see

a couple of wrinkles on your face, too." His sister was so vain he expected her to grab a mirror.

"In your dreams, old man."

"Learn to cook," his uncle said to Gail, "and the men will come."

She rolled her eyes. "You are one sorry man. I don't know how Aunt Helen puts up with you."

"By ignoring him," his aunt said, dishing a second helping of fried chicken.

Drake's mind flashed to Jasmine again.

"It's going to take you forever to get some grandkids, sis," his uncle said. "Grandkids are pure joy."

The macaroni stuck in Drake's throat. He swallowed three times before he choked it down.

They'd had this same conversation around the dining-room table a million times. Babies weren't something men often talked about. It was just a given that after you were married a few years and settled down a couple of kids would come along. Drake's fork clattered on his plate.

"Deanna is home for the weekend," Gail said just to pester him. "She's living in D.C. now. I invited her over. She should be here in an hour."

"You two used to hang out together," Drake said.

"But she's not coming to see your sister. She's

here to see you," his mother said. "I don't think you've seen her in five or six years. Very attractive young lady." Now his mother was on the marriage bandwagon.

"You're not trying to choose my dates for me, are you, Mom? I thought you gave up a long time ago."

"Mothers never give up, son. I just want to see you settled with a nice young lady. Your dad and I were married at your age and you're not even seriously dating someone."

"Well, I like to take my time," Drake said. "It's a serious decision and I certainly don't want to be included in the fifty percent divorce rate."

"Bite your tongue, young man. I'll say the problem is instant gratification. Couples aren't willing to put in the time to iron out the kinks."

"Some aren't worth ironing out."

"Some could survive if they gave themselves more time and stopped looking for the image of the ones on TV. No one's perfect. There's that adjustment period."

"How did we get on this topic?" Gail asked. "It's soooo depressing."

"I agree," Drake said. What woman would want to marry a man who couldn't give her children?

The conversation had made dinner stressful. Soon after dinner, Gail's friend arrived, but she wasn't Jasmine. They talked over old times before Deanna finally went to the movies with his sister and he drove back to Middleburg earlier than he'd planned.

Against his better wishes, Drake called Jasmine. He'd ask her out on a date. For dinner or maybe a movie or show, something. But she didn't answer her phone.

Jasmine had just come in from an emergency call. Floyd was on call, but the vet tech said he was already handling an emergency. So he asked if she would take the call. Just as she was walking in the door, Casey called to her.

"Hey, girl."

Jasmine waved.

"Noelle and I are going shopping at Tysons Corner. Want to go with us?"

"Just got in from a call."

"She won't be here for at least half an hour. You have time to dress. Come on. It'll be fun. We'll have dinner before we come home."

Maybe it would be good to hang out with other women. She needed to be more sociable. Also it gave her more time with her sister. Jasmine shook her head. She still couldn't wrap her mind around that.

"All right."

Jasmine showered and dressed in record time. She was ready by the time Noelle drove up in her sporty little car. Noelle tooted her horn. Casey and Jasmine came out at the same time. But Jasmine's steps slowed. Since Noelle didn't invite her, she felt as if she were imposing.

Noelle hopped out of the car. "I'm glad you could come, Jasmine."

Casey slid in the backseat and Jasmine slid into the front passenger seat. "I only do this once," Casey said. "Next time, you're in the back."

"I don't care where I sit as long as I don't have to drive. I feel like I spend most of my life on the road."

"I never thought about that. You have to drive from farm to farm. How far do you go each day?"

"An average of one hundred to one hundred and fifty miles, depending on my caseload."

"That has to be a pain," Casey said.

"Not really. It's beautiful out here. The scenery relaxes me."

"You can see more of it if you didn't have to drive. Dr. Floyd usually lets the vet tech drive."

"I think he's the only one with a tech right now," Jasmine said.

"Well, just sit back and enjoy," Noelle said. "We'll be at the shopping center before you know it."

Noelle's little car shot forward. The serene mountain roads gently gave way to more lanes and more traffic. It was immediately apparent when they were nearing the city. People drove as if they were trying out to be racecar drivers, shooting in and out of lanes as if they were afraid of missing something. It reminded her of L.A.

Finally they pulled into a crowded area, the likes of which Jasmine hadn't seen since she'd arrived in Virginia.

Noelle circled a while before she fought for a suitable parking space in the mall parking lot.

Tysons Mall had lots of high-end stores.

"So what are you shopping for?" Jasmine asked.

"We don't know," Noelle said. "Maybe a few things to wear on the honeymoon, but I have a few months. I'm not rushed. I just love to shop. I could use a new purse."

An hour into shopping, Jasmine wondered why she had wasted a perfectly good afternoon. They took loads of clothes into the changing room, didn't buy one single item, then they found another handful of clothes to try. Jasmine was slowly going insane. Were she and Noelle really sisters? She was seriously contemplating taking a taxi back home. She didn't care about the cost.

"Jasmine, try this on," Noelle said.

"What?"

"Try it on," said Casey.

Jasmine fingered the thin, skimpy blouse as if it were a foreign object. "We're looking for clothes for Noelle. We don't have time to shop for me."

"I don't know what I'm looking for," Noelle said. "You're the only one who hasn't tried anything on. Come on."

Jasmine shook her head. That blouse definitely wasn't her.

"Come on. Is this your size?"

Jasmine checked the label and nodded.

"Then let's go." They finagled Jasmine into a dressing room. Before she could try on the blouse, a pair of slacks sailed across the door.

"Open up so we can see it," Noelle said after a few minutes.

By the time Jasmine modeled the first outfit, they had three more outfits for her to try.

"I'm not trying on all these clothes."

"Won't take but a minute," Noelle said. "That outfit looks great on you. You *have* to get it."

Jasmine had to agree it looked fabulous on her curves.

"You have to strut your stuff," Casey said. "With the clothes you wear, a man wouldn't know you had curves at all. They like women with hips and a butt. You have enough to give a man whiplash."

Jasmine laughed. "You need to stop." She didn't turn heads. "The horses don't care what I wear."

"You aren't trying to impress the horses, girlfriend," Casey said.

She would not think of Drake. She hadn't heard from him at all after the kiss that left her tossing and turning in her bed late into the night.

She tried on the other outfits they handed her.

"I don't know how you could leave any of these in the store," Noelle said. "They look fabulous on you. And then you won't have to go shopping when Drake asks you out."

Jasmine groaned, "You all are too much." But she left the store with four new outfits.

Jasmine couldn't believe it. She gazed at Noelle and Casey. They were treating her as if they'd been friends for years. They were accepting her for who she was.

"I have enough food at home to feed a stable of horses," Noelle said. "Let's eat at my place."

Noelle's house was an old white colonial. Farther back, some distance away, hidden by trees, stood several buildings.

"Leila sent over some of the leftovers from the party. I have enough food to last all of us a couple of weeks, so I'm going to pack enough for you to take home with you," Noelle said. "I think Grandpa is afraid I'll melt away. He's always asking Leila to make sure my refrigerator is stocked."

"He probably indulges all of your whims," Jasmine said.

"He's the perfect granddad now, but it's no secret that I didn't grow up here," Noelle said. "I moved here in January."

Jasmine nodded, but wouldn't ask her to explain. Jasmine knew Noelle's parents lived in California.

Noelle smiled. "I just learned recently that George Avery *was* my grandfather. I came here to meet him. Many of the people around here know my background," she said. "My mother and Mackenzie Avery were childhood neighbors and close friends. When my father found out he was sterile, my mother asked Mackenzie Avery to be the donor. He was in school in California then.

And his features were very much like my father's. He saw how badly my mom and dad wanted children, and wanted to help."

Jasmine understood the reason Mackenzie had donated sperm for Jasmine's parents, but why did he do it for a virtual stranger? She would never know the answer.

She stared and Noelle continued to talk.

"I know. Crazy story, right? It seems so odd. My grandfather didn't know of my existence and he was grieving after Mackenzie died. When I arrived, shortly after I learned the truth, I didn't know whether I'd even identify myself. But Colin convinced me to do so. Colin impressed upon me that my grandfather needed me, and so we told him together." She glanced at a picture of the older man, who was barely smiling about something. "I'm glad I did. It's changed him. Gave him something to live for."

Deep into thoughts of George Avery and Noelle's story, Jasmine jumped when Casey's arm touched hers. Noelle seemed so well adjusted.

"How did you learn about Mackenzie?" Jasmine asked.

"My parents told me years ago, but I was older when I developed this yearning to meet him."

"How did your parents feel about all this?"

"My dad and Granddad play poker and golf together. Granddad is actually going to Carmel in a couple of weeks to play a few rounds and watch Tiger Woods play at Pebble Beach."

"So you had a good relationship with your father."

"The best. Truthfully, I'm a daddy's girl. Mackenzie was dead by the time I was ready to meet him. My mother's parents ran a summer camp here when I was small. The one I'm reopening this summer, and this is their old house. Anyway, Mackenzie gave me riding lessons when I was small. I didn't know of our connection then, but he did."

Suddenly a shadow crossed Noelle's face. "We talked the week before he died, and we were going to get together that weekend. Both of us were looking forward to the trip."

"He wanted to get to know you as an adult?"

"Very much."

Noelle was conceived just like she was. A million questions ran through Jasmine's mind.

"How did your dad feel about this?"

"I don't know how he would have felt if Mackenzie was still alive. He knew I was going to spend time with Mackenzie, and then after his death, come here to meet my grandfather. By then

Mackenzie wasn't a threat to him. Like I said, I'm Daddy's girl."

Daddy's girl. What would it feel like to be Daddy's girl?

Jasmine cleared her throat. "I'm sorry you didn't get to see Mackenzie before his death."

"Yes," Noelle said quietly, her eyes becoming glassy. "Me, too."

Jasmine stood. "I'll set the table while you get the food." She had to move, do something other than sit and think.

Two hours later, Noelle took Jasmine and Casey home. Jasmine barely had time to get inside before her phone rang.

"Jasmine…"

"Drake, could you come over?"

"Sure. I'm twenty minutes away, but I'll be right there."

What would happen if she told Mr. Avery she was his granddaughter? Would he want her? Would he trust her as easily as he trusted Noelle? Noelle had a family connection. Her mother was a neighbor. Jasmine was a stranger. How could he welcome a stranger as easily?

Jasmine scrubbed her hand over her face. Why did she ask Drake to come over? He couldn't do anything. It was a spur-of-the-moment decision, when her defenses were down. But she was glad he was coming. She did not want to be alone.

Jasmine sounded panicked. Drake mashed on the gas. All kinds of disasters ran through his head in the fifteen minutes it took him to get to her place. He'd sped all the way.

She met him at the door. When she fell into his arms, he was as shocked as she seemed to be. Anything that would make this strong woman come unglued was serious.

"What's wrong?" he asked.

Gathering her strength, she pulled back. "I'm sorry I called you over. I'm okay."

"What's wrong?" he repeated, easing her into the room and closing the door.

"I'm just being silly."

He took her face between his hands and gazed directly in her eyes. "Talk to me, Jasmine. Trust me."

She turned away, led the way to the family room. "I just keep thinking about Mr. Avery. He's my grandfather, too, but I can't tell him."

"Why not?"

"There's the drama with his nephew. Then there's the trouble at the office. If people found out they'll think I'm looking for a handout. That I expect special treatment because of our connection."

"No, they won't. You pull your own weight and then some."

"People get funny when money and careers are involved. I've worked too hard to get where I am to have my work second-guessed."

"You have to tell him eventually. Don't you see? If he accepted Noelle, he'll accept you, too."

"It's too much all at once. He only found out about Noelle. I can't just spring myself on him immediately. Maybe in a year or two."

"Think about it, Jasmine. You have a newfound sister and a grandfather. They would willingly accept you in the fold."

"I don't know that. At least, I'm not ready to test it."

This was tearing her apart and Drake wanted to help her. "You don't have to make the decision today."

Their gazes met. "No. I'll be here for a while. You're right. I have time."

As if it were as natural as rain, she came to him, slid her arms around his waist and lay her head against his chest. Drake closed his arms around her.

He wanted her. Really wanted her. He'd only have to move a few inches for his lips to touch hers. But she didn't need a lover right now. She needed friendship. And if it killed him, and Lord knew it was, friendship was what he'd give her.

For now.

Chapter 5

Although Jasmine liked to drive to appointments to enjoy the solitude between visits, the vet assistant was driving her around today. With Ponce on vacation, her workday was extremely long. Floyd had suggested she take the intern. She pulled out her BlackBerry and started to write up notes on her visits. This way she wouldn't have to do it once she got back to the office. She closed her eyes a moment to gather her thoughts. Her day had started at four-thirty that morning. It was already five in the afternoon and she had another three hours to go—at least.

"I really like this work," the vet assistant, Gordon Dale, said. "I'm looking forward to becoming a vet one day."

Jasmine smiled. It had been only a couple of years since she was at his stage. But it seemed like a lifetime ago. Where had the time gone? You really had to like the work to put in the long, dirty hours. At least he was competent.

"It won't be long," she said. "Where are you from?"

"New York."

"Do you want to practice there?"

He shrugged. "Not sure. I want to roam around a little first. Maybe even go to a foreign country. Work on an African safari or something."

"Sounds exciting. Especially since a lot of the animals are becoming extinct. I have a friend over there now."

"Yeah. That's cool. How much farther to the next stop?"

"Another fifteen minutes."

"I guess you cover a lot of territory working in a rural area like this."

"We cover farms in a fifty-mile radius. Travel over all kinds of roads."

Jasmine's mother had called the day before.

She usually called twice a week. This time she told Jasmine again that she and her stepfather would be arriving soon—as if Jasmine needed the reminder. Time to get busy finding a bedroom set for the guest bedroom. As if she had the time to shop.

More than likely Steven would come with them since Drake was his friend. Maybe he'd stay at Drake's place.

Drake. If that wasn't another kettle of trouble, she didn't know what was. That kiss. She still couldn't get it out of her mind. He'd called her Sunday to take her out to dinner, but she'd refused. Instead she'd fallen in his arms like an airhead with no self-esteem or coping skills. Suddenly she'd lost her ability to think. That's exactly what he must be thinking.

They needed distance, which wasn't difficult. It was Wednesday, and she'd managed to avoid him since Sunday. In a sense she felt ungrateful, like a coward. He'd canceled his date to take her to Noelle's party. And she hadn't thanked him for it. He'd brought over dinner many evenings to make her feel more welcome.

Pensively, she gazed out the window. She suffered the dull ache of desire at the thought of him. And she hungered from the memory of his mouth on hers—from the contact of his body pressed against her.

Okay, okay. She'd take him to dinner. Jasmine sighed. When was the last time she'd enjoyed herself with a man? Too long, she thought. Would a relationship with Drake be so bad? But they were coworkers. They were friends.

"You tired?"

"No." They'd made it to the next farm. Drake would have eaten long before she finished work.

"What do you think is wrong with it?" Jasmine asked Drake. It was after six and she had one more stop to make. Of course her stupid truck chose to break down now.

Drake dragged his head from under the hood long enough to say, "Haven't got a clue. The tow truck should be here soon."

"Probably too late to rent something tonight."

"Take my truck," he said. "After you drop me off at home."

"How would you get to work?"

"I'll catch a ride from one of my neighbors. No problem. I'm in the office all day."

He didn't have to do that, but this was the

Drake she'd come to know and appreciate. "Thanks," she said.

They started moving the contents of Jasmine's truck into Drake's. His was a newer model than hers and a lot cleaner. They'd finished by the time the tow truck pulled up and attached her truck for a trip to the local garage.

Drake drove them to the last appointment, which went quicker with his help. From there, they went to the office.

"Hey, Gordon, can you unpack for Jasmine?" Drake asked. "Then join us inside. I have dinner."

"Sure," the young man said, eyes lighting up at the mention of food. Jasmine would have let him off the hook, but he hadn't come in before noon while she'd already put in a full day's work by then. They should have stopped for something to eat before returning to the office. But Jasmine just wanted to go home, shower and go to bed.

Jasmine followed Drake into the office.

"What do you want to talk to me about?" she asked.

"I have your dinner."

"I can eat after we talk. What's up?"

"I'm hungry. I'm going to eat."

She detoured to the bathroom to wash up. Then they sat in the reception area and ate.

"What did you want to talk to me about?" she asked once she'd eaten enough to take the edge off her hunger.

"Just wanted to see if you were eating properly. And you aren't."

"Ponce will be back on Sunday. Life will go back to normal."

"You mean, your normal twelve-hour days instead of sixteen and seventeen hours?"

Jasmine shrugged and bit into the fish and moaned. "I was just thinking I owe you dinner. You've been so kind to me."

He leaned against the counter, crossed his arms. "You don't owe me anything."

She forked up another bite and chewed. "I owe you an apology. For falling all over you Sunday and avoiding you afterward. I had a lot of thinking to do."

"And did you come up with some conclusion?"

He looked too damn good standing there. If Jasmine weren't so hungry she would have lost her appetite with the emotions swirling through her. She should be used to him by now.

He sauntered toward her and eased his tall frame into the seat beside her. Her heart somersaulted.

The fork clinked on the plate. She looked down. The succulent fish was the last thought on her mind.

He'd showered, she noticed, when she got a whiff of the citrus cologne or soap. Whatever. He smelled like heaven while she had a day-old horse scent. Why would he want to be anywhere near her?

He stretched his arms along the back of the sofa and positioned his ankle on his thigh.

"Aren't you going to eat?"

"I ate earlier."

Jasmine nodded.

"The office needs another large-animal vet, maybe two," Drake said. "Even with the two of you working, your caseload is too large."

"I agree. I don't know how they kept up before I arrived."

"We had a temporary for a while. He left a couple of weeks before you arrived. If you keep this up you'll need one, too. Floyd is bringing in new business all the time."

"We can discuss it at the next office meeting," Jasmine said. Drake had a point. "Although it will slow down after most of the foals have arrived next month."

"Not by much. There's always something."

Jasmine finished her food. "I hate to eat and run, but I've got another long day tomorrow."

"That's if you don't get any calls tonight."

"God forbid." Standing, Jasmine made her way to the door.

"You have Monday off, don't you?"

Jasmine nodded around a yawn.

"I'd like to take you to dinner."

"I have to shop for furniture. I'll take you if I can find everything Sunday."

Drake shook his head. "Eating out of a carton doesn't constitute a date."

Date? "Ah, Drake."

He closed the distance between them, lowered his head and kissed her. It was as dizzying as it had been the first time, but she attributed this time to fatigue. He was romancing her in her weakest state.

She pressed a hand against his warm chest and inhaled the attractive citrus scent.

"This can't work," she mumbled into his chest.

"Why not? Because your kiss tells me differently."

"We've got history."

"No, we don't."

"You and Steve…"

"Honey, we're way past that argument. Steve

has nothing to do with the way we feel. He's in L.A. We're here and what's between us hasn't got a damn thing to do with home."

"I wish it were that easy."

"It is." He lowered his head again and kissed her.

Jasmine should stop him, but she found herself dragging her hands around to his back and pressing him close to her. Her calm was shattered with the hunger of his kiss. Her nipples hardened and pressed against his warmth. She knew that once her mind cleared, once the fatigue wore off, she'd feel like an idiot. But now… God, but now, he felt like heaven at the end of a hellish day. She kissed him back with a hunger that belied her earlier caution.

"Want me to go home with you and tuck you in?"

Jasmine jerked back. The image was much too enticing.

"I think I can handle that." Slowly but surely, he was worming his way into her heart.

"Okay, you can drop me off at my house and take the car."

"Thanks."

"And if your car isn't out of the shop by Sunday I'll go shopping with you."

"I thought men hated to shop."

"Depends on who we're with."

They made their way to the car. Drake tossed his keys to her and headed to the passenger seat. As Jasmine climbed in and started the motor a thousand what-ifs ran through her mind.

Maybe it was time she let go and enjoy. From the time she was a child she'd been on guard practically every wakeful moment. Could she afford to let her guard down now? Would Drake drag her heart through the mud before it was all over? Was he really as good as he seemed, or was he a wolf in sheep's clothing?

Jasmine was at River Oaks.

Mr. Avery was at a race one of their horses was competing in and hadn't returned yet. She'd like to know his history. How he came to own the farm. What his childhood had been like. The kind of genes running on his side of the family. She wanted to know about Mackenzie, too, and his mother.

Jasmine's mother always called her stubborn to a fault. She wondered who that trait came from.

It was Sunday and Maggie Girl was colicky, and Jasmine was fighting to save her. Since she was pregnant, they were concerned about losing both the horse and the fetus.

Jasmine rushed into the stable. Maggie Girl was on the floor, thrashing.

"How long has she been like this?" Jasmine asked.

"Little over an hour," Burt said. "I gave her some medicine, but it didn't work."

He and Colin were on the barn floor trying to soothe the animal, but they weren't having much luck.

Burt called over a couple of hands to hold her still while Jasmine gave her medication.

Jasmine took out a syringe, filled it with medication and clamped it between her teeth. The horse was thrashing about so much she had a devil of a time inserting the needle. The last thing she needed was for the needle to break.

"You've got to hold her still."

"Get over here, now!" Burt hollered and a couple of hands came running in. With the four of them holding on to the horse, she got the needle in. Jasmine patted her side to try to soothe the animal and give the medicine time to work. With the way she was struggling, Maggie Girl would be lucky to hold on to the fetus.

Three hours later, Maggie Girl was on her

feet. Jasmine did an ultrasound to make sure the fetus was okay.

When she was ready to leave, Noelle approached her. "I know this was supposed to be your day off. Let me take you to lunch."

Jasmine glanced at her watch. "I need to get cleaned up. Drake's taking me furniture shopping. My mother's coming in a couple weeks."

"We're about the same size. You can clean up here, saving you the time of going back home. We can eat at the house. Leila always has something cooking."

"Thanks, but I need to get moving."

"I heard your car's in the shop. If you need to go shopping during the week, let me know. Shopping takes time, what with the furniture, choosing matching pillows, prints for the walls, decorating pieces and spreads."

Jasmine eyes widened as the list grew longer. She held up a hand.

Noelle nodded at Jasmine's stricken expression. "Thought so. You aren't going to finish everything today."

"Not now, since you've named a million items I hadn't thought of."

"Please. I really want to spend more time with

you. Maggie Girl means so much to Colin. He chose her. And she's carrying my foal. Let me thank you. Besides, it's always more fun shopping with another woman. What do men know about decorating?"

Given that her enormous vet fee would be plenty of compensation, Noelle looked as if she really wanted to spend the day with Jasmine. Besides, it would keep her mind off the date with Drake.

"I'm off on Monday if you're available. I'm hoping I'll have my car back by then," Jasmine finally said. She'd worked fourteen days without a break. She was finally getting a day off.

"I'm looking forward to it," Noelle said as if it were a foregone conclusion.

Back at home, Jasmine peeled off her clothing and got into the shower using the scented soap she'd purchased on her shopping spree that weekend. It felt heavenly to be so clean. She dressed in the lovely teal top with jeans and a new pair of underwear with a matching bra.

Hugs barked when he greeted the animals in the barn.

"Easy, girl," Drake warned. Hugs's health had

improved immensely and she was getting friskier by the day. Kelly, Drake's neighbor, had ridden her bicycle to his house the other day wanting to play with the dog. She still longed to take Hugs home with her.

Drake was getting attached to the dog. Hugs went home with him each night. Everyone regarded her as his dog now. At this point, he guessed she was.

Drake spent an hour in the barn checking injuries and playing with the healthy animals. Then he went into the office and dialed Jasmine's number. When she didn't answer he tried her cell phone.

"Hi. Enjoy your morning in?" he asked.

"I've been at work since eight."

"Why?"

She told him about the emergency at River Oaks.

"Why didn't Floyd take it?"

"I'm on call. He was on call yesterday, remember?"

"Ready to go shopping?"

"No, but it can't be helped."

Drake chuckled. "I miss you."

A long sigh, then, "I miss you, too. I'll see you in a few minutes."

Drake slowly hung up. His mind never strayed very far from Jasmine—and the hot kisses they shared. Their relationship seemed doomed before it began. He liked her. Never in a million years did he think he'd have feelings for a woman like Jasmine. Especially since he knew her from way back. She'd turned into quite a woman.

But he couldn't have children. He couldn't forget that. So why was he obsessing over her? Why couldn't he leave her the heck alone?

When he read the schedule for Monday, he realized his first project was a neutering. He inhaled deeply. Sterilization was a normal procedure for any vet. It was needed. It was unfair having so many homeless animals around getting hit by cars or starving. With the city crowding the land, there just wasn't a safe place for animals any longer. So he guessed it was the more humane thing to do.

But he didn't have to like it.

Everything brought him reluctantly back to Jasmine. He was falling for her in a way he never expected to. He couldn't afford to let himself continue down that path. Their relationship was a foregone conclusion. She wanted children by a man who could give them to her. He couldn't.

But he wanted to help her. The quickest way to

do that was to get her to reveal her identity to Mr. Avery. He couldn't betray her. He wasn't going to tell the old man. The only solution was to convince her to do so.

When Jasmine walked into the office, Drake's eyes skimmed her body from head to toe zapping her with laser beams of pure heat.

Jasmine was accustomed to the cheerleaders and popular girls in school getting those looks, but she wasn't accustomed to having them aimed at her.

It felt good. Damn good to know a man thought you were so attractive he was rendered speechless.

Thank you, Noelle and Casey.

"So, is this the product of your shopping spree?" he asked, slowly strolling toward her.

Jasmine tugged at her blouse. "Yes." She couldn't take her eyes off him. When he stopped, he brushed up against her. He lifted his hand, smoothing it along her arm. Her stomach dipped.

"You need to shop more often."

"Umm. Ready?"

One of the vet techs took that moment to come in with Hugs. Drake put a little distance between them, but the heat in his eyes stayed with her.

"So what are you looking for?" Drake asked.

Jasmine cleared her throat. "Let's see. I need a couch for the living room and a bedroom set for the guest room, for starters."

Hugs came over for a pat and Jasmine reached out to stroke her.

"What are you going to do with Hugs? It's too hot to leave her in the car today."

"I'm leaving her here with the tech." He stroked the dog before he led Jasmine outside. When the door closed, Hugs looked as if they were deserting her.

"We'll be back soon, Hugs," Jasmine said as they made their way to the truck.

"So where were you thinking of going?" They piled into the truck. Drake drove this time. She'd cleaned up his truck before she'd dressed.

Jasmine named a couple of places she'd shopped at before and Drake made suggestions. But she knew neither of them was thinking about shopping. When she got within ten feet of him, she wanted to take him to bed.

Jasmine reached for a bottle of water, but Drake grabbed her hand.

"Have you thought any more about revealing your identity to your grandfather?" he asked.

"I've thought about it a lot, but I'm not going to tell him."

"It's your reason for being here. He can give you what you never found with your father."

"If he accepts me."

"Are you afraid he won't?"

"There's the possibility."

"Why would he accept Noelle and not you? You're as much his granddaughter as Noelle. She would be the sister you never had."

"This isn't a fairy tale. My life isn't going to be magically fixed if I tell him."

"No. But sometimes you see problems instead of opportunities. You can build a meaningful relationship with him and your reason for being here will be accomplished. But you can't do any of that unless you tell him."

"No."

Drake's hand clenched around the steering wheel. "You are one stubborn woman."

Jasmine glimpsed his profile. He had some nerve. "I'm sure Steven has told you that."

"Yes, but I don't believe everything he tells me." Drake said, then fell silent, giving Jasmine a chance to think.

"Why is it so important to you?"

"I'm not the issue here. That connection is important to you."

The truth was, while she wasn't afraid to tussle with a large horse, or a cow that could crush her, she was afraid of not being accepted once again.

When her father and mother divorced, she'd called him daily. Half the time he'd talk to her a minute or two before he gave her some excuse to sever the connection. He broke the connection so many times, she'd stopped calling. It had taken her way too long to get the message. Her father just didn't want her. She wasn't going to lay her heart on the line again—not ever—for some man to crush it to a pulp.

She didn't *need* Mr. Avery. Hadn't she literally taken care of herself since she graduated from high school? No, she didn't need anyone. She'd just wanted to meet him. And she wasn't sweet Noelle.

Besides, her mother had told her not to impose on that family. But when did she listen to her mother?

"How long are you going to keep tormenting both of us?" Drake said, dragging her attention back to him.

"Tormenting you?"

"Just forget it."

"I can't. What are you talking about?"

"We're here." He maneuvered the truck in the turn lane and pulled into the shopping area.

She was tormenting him?

Drake let Hugs out to run after breakfast. He had another half hour before it was time to leave for work. He nursed his cup of coffee thinking of Jasmine. When they'd finished shopping the day before, she'd dropped him off at his house and, like a fool, he'd invited her in. Although she wasn't working, he let her keep his truck so she could do whatever women did on their days off.

He'd wanted to take her to bed so badly he ached. And he couldn't forget the question on her face when she was so obviously willing to take their relationship to another level. But he wouldn't go there.

Hugs started to bark excitedly and Drake went out to see what was wrong.

Marsha and Kelly were walking their two dogs along the road. Then Drake's cell phone rang. It was Steven. He let it go to voice mail. Steven had been making a pest out of himself lately.

Hugs no longer used the cage. She was still a little sore and wasn't up to her normal energy level.

"Oh, there's Hugs," Kelly said, running toward them.

"She's a lot better," Drake said.

"Can I pet her?"

"Sure you can."

The little girl reached out and Hugs, a definite people lover, snuggled up to her.

Drake leaned against the car as the two played. Marsha approached him holding the leashes of their two champion show dogs. Two golden retrievers bouncing around wanting to play, too, but Marsha barked out an order and they obeyed like the well-trained beasts they were.

"Take Hugs around the side, honey, so these two will calm down." Marsha reached down and patted them as they sat on the ground.

"Do you need a ride to work?" she asked.

"Sure, thanks."

"I'm going that way anyway. I wanted to talk to you about a fund-raising event for the animals you keep. It occurred to me that you're building quite a menagerie in that old barn. And upkeep costs money."

"That's for sure."

"Are you able to find homes for many of them?"

Drake shook his head. "We have a few birds

that can't fly. They'll be here permanently unless we can find a home for them. And an assorted group of dogs, cats, birds and stray wild animals."

Thinking of the school loans he was still paying off, a little aid in that department would be a tremendous help. So far the expenses were all out of his pocket. He was grateful the techs and Floyd gave their time off the clock.

"Well, I'm the fund-raising queen. I'll write up a proposal and show it to you. And also there are plenty of people who wouldn't mind volunteering their time to help you."

"I appreciate that, Marsha."

"Mom, Hugs is a lot better," Kelly said. "Can we take her home now?"

"No, sweetheart. We have all we can handle right here."

Jasmine couldn't help thinking that shopping with Noelle was a whole new experience. Most of Jasmine's friends had been like her. They weren't shopaholics. They always found other things to occupy their time.

Noelle hopped out of the truck. Slowly, Jasmine followed. They were half sisters. She and her sister were spending the afternoon together.

How many times had she wanted this as a teenager? Suddenly shopping wasn't so bad after all. Not bad at all.

"Hey, what's your favorite color?" Noelle asked.

"Red."

"So we'll do something in the red family for your bedroom. How does that sound?"

"Just a little red. Or else I'll be in a fighting mood."

"How about red and green. Green's relaxing. We'll just have a touch of red."

Earlier Noelle had dragged her to the paint store for paint samples to help choose colors. She had them in her hand now.

"Maybe something calming for the guest room. Something in the blue family?"

"Sounds good."

"We're going to make the guest room a retreat with candles, pretty pillows."

"My mother would love that." As much as Jasmine fought with her mother, she didn't dislike her. She loved her. It was the baggage that came with her that drove Jasmine crazy. Her mother did so much for everyone that she took little time for herself and usually little time for her daughter. She needed a retreat. She should have left Norman at home.

By the time they finished in one store, Jasmine was sure they'd bought the place out. They had pillows, pictures and candles.

"If you were more of a shopper, I would have shopped several stores for things, but knowing you, I'd never get you out again."

"That's the truth," Jasmine said, wondering if they shared any genetic traits at all.

"And we still have a few more things to purchase for the guest room."

"I have one more afternoon off and I'm not spending it shopping."

"Lord forbid. I'll do it on my own. It'll be easier anyway. Is that okay with you?"

"Fine, fine."

Noelle shook her head.

Jasmine started to sling the bags in the back, but stopped when she remembered the cost and precious time it took to purchase them.

They had even added some things for the bathroom, such as candles, pretty linens and towels.

"It shouldn't take long to get your room set up," Noelle said.

"I hope not."

"Drake will appreciate it."

"He hasn't made it past the family room."

"Honey, eventually he's going to make it upstairs and I'm going to make sure you dazzle him."

Jasmine rolled her eyes and laughed. "You're too much." But the idea of Drake coming upstairs had been on her mind lately.

"Honestly, Jasmine, I don't know how anyone your age coming out of L.A. is so clueless about fashion." Her tone was rife with exasperation.

"Fashion wasn't exactly at the top of my list when I lived there."

Noelle snorted delicately. "That's obvious."

Chapter 6

During the couple of minutes Drake took for lunch the next day, he headed to the makeshift home for the animals. He was surprised to see Floyd already there checking one of the injured ones.

Drake eased his hands into his pockets. "I thought you were out on your calls."

"Had one close by so I decided to take my lunch break here," Floyd said.

The older man rarely spent time in the office, especially this time of day.

"Looks like this one will be flying again soon," he said of the bird.

"Coming along nicely."

"I've known you for how many months now?" Floyd asked, sparing a brief glance at Drake before he focused on the bird again.

Drake chuckled, wondering where Floyd was going with this. "Almost a year."

"You're not the same easygoing person I'm accustomed to seeing. You look stressed out. I recognized the signs a few weeks ago, but I thought it was just something you had to work through."

Did it show that much? His problem had been weighing heavily on his mind, but he didn't want the whole damn world to know. And he certainly didn't want to talk about it.

"I know you were sick a couple of months ago, but that's all over now."

Drake nodded. "I'm fine."

"So what could it be?" Hugs sidled up to Floyd and he reached out to ruffle the dog's fur. "I'm a good listener, Drake. If you feel you need to talk, I'm here. I know in some respects you're new, but you're not alone."

"Just had some bad news I have to learn to live with, that's all."

"Sometimes it's easier when you share. Whatever you say stays with me."

The chuckle that Drake emitted was dry and uneasy. "I've said the same thing to someone else lately with the hopes that person would trust me."

"Two-way street," Floyd said, then deliberately paused. "Maybe you need to trust someone, too."

"I discovered I'm sterile from the mumps." Drake couldn't believe he'd blurted it right out.

"I'm sorry, man."

"I wasn't even thinking about having children, just figured it would happen one day when I married. Now…"

"There are many more options now. There's artificial insemination."

"Except that might be a problem with the woman I'm interested in. I haven't told her and I don't know what will happen to the relationship when I do."

"Those kinds of secrets aren't good. If your relationship is meant to be, she'll understand," he said. "Are the two of you serious?"

He shook his head. "Not formally, at least not yet, but I want it to go there."

"Before it goes too far you should tell her. And it's not the end of the world. Medical science has progressed a lot with fertility research in the past few years. There are other options."

Drake nodded.

"Look, I won't brush your feelings aside as if they don't matter, because they do. But I wouldn't give up on a relationship for that reason. Finding the right fit is tough. When you come down to it, it's you and her. Sure you want kids, but the hard part is just getting the two of you to work. So try concentrating on that right now. Worry about the children later."

Floyd glanced at his watch. "Call me when you need to talk, okay? You don't have to wait for me to read your mind."

Drake nodded.

"I'm serious. It's not good keeping pain all bottled up."

"I will, and thanks."

Drake called Hugs and started to the office.

"Drake?" Floyd called out.

"Yes?" Drake turned to face the older man.

"Is she worth fighting for?"

As prickly as the feisty Jasmine could be, he could definitely be content with her. The question was easy to answer. "Yes."

"Then I guess you have your answer."

It was easy saying the words, but convincing Jasmine that he was worth taking a chance on was a totally different thing.

If she were any other woman, he'd have a chance. But Jasmine had a host of problems of her own that would not be easy to overcome.

Floyd was walking toward the door when he faced Drake. "You're still a great man," he said. "You've got heart and that hasn't changed."

Heart. Was heart enough? Drake wondered as he walked back toward the office. He was sure Jasmine's father had plenty of heart in the beginning until it all started eating away at him. What did it do to a man to know his wife wanted children and he was incapable of providing her with them?

What was the measure of a man?

Jasmine could not believe she'd let Noelle talk her into shopping again. If it wasn't for the fact her mother's arrival loomed, she'd tell Noelle to forget it, sister or not. She'd gotten her truck out of the shop last evening. She was grateful for her own transportation, though she liked Drake's ride better.

"So what are you looking for?" Noelle asked.

"Let's see. Drake and I picked out the living-room couch and bedroom set over the weekend. They're delivering them this week."

She'd worked seven hours and had eaten a late

lunch at the Avery place. Mr. Avery came back from his trip in time to join them.

"Why don't you all take my truck just in case you want to bring back larger items that won't fit comfortably in yours," Mr. Avery said. "Some of the men here can lift heavy things for you. I don't want you girls lifting anything."

"Thanks," Jasmine said.

"Sorry we can't help you with furniture. We gave away all our old things when Leila decided to redecorate. Buying furniture is a real chore."

Jasmine shook her head. "You can say that again, but I have the pieces I need."

"Shopping is fun, Granddad."

He placed an arm around Noelle's shoulder. "You all enjoy yourselves. You've got a real shopper with Noelle. Woman loves it."

"I'm glad somebody does," Jasmine said.

"You take after me, then, because I can't think of a worse way to spend the day. You all have fun."

Jasmine's eyes strayed to Mr. Avery. *You take after me. Did she?*

"We'll have plenty of fun," Noelle said, and the two of them left. "So tell me where were you thinking of going?" They piled into a farm truck with both the front and backseat.

"We still have lots of shopping to do before the entire house is fully decorated. Do we need to shop for clothes, too?"

"I can't believe I let you talk me into buying all those clothes."

"I'd like to get a look at your wardrobe "

"I bet you would," Jasmine mumble ʒ-mined to keep Noelle away from her close.

"You're a high-powered vet who handles multi-million-dollar animals. You should dress the part."

"I do. I won't wear silk to wrestle in a stall."

Noelle merely shook her head. "Your entire life isn't spent in the stall. You have to do something so Drake will think of you as more of a woman and less of a vet."

"He's a vet, too. He understands."

"Honey, he's a man."

Jasmine didn't have a rebuttal. He certainly was a man.

"Remember when the furniture is delivered you have to check and make sure there are no scrapes on the legs or anywhere. Any particular way you want it set up?"

"Only one way for it to fit in the bedroom. There are a couple of options for the living area."

"Mind if I take a look?"

"Knock yourself out," Jasmine said.

"Do you have a bedspread for your bedroom?"

"No. Only the blankets my mother sent for the other place but I haven't taken the time to shop for anything else."

"We should pass a home store in the next block. We can take a quick look at spreads and pillows."

It was just too much bother working fifteen- and sixteen-hour days and having to worry about decorating. What a way to spend an afternoon.

Quickly, Jasmine exited the car. The quicker they chose what she needed, the quicker she'd go home. She stopped in midstep.

She and her sister—*sister*—were spending more time together. She smiled. Maybe it wouldn't be so bad.

Drake didn't have a clue what to expect when he picked Jasmine up. He hoped she wore one of those sexy little numbers like the day before. He'd planned the evening well. Nothing to make her feel on edge. They were two friends spending the evening together.

Yeah, and he could talk himself into believing the sky was falling. Friendship didn't touch what he felt for Jasmine.

When he met her at her door, she was dressed in a knockout royal-blue top. She looked nothing like the vet in baggy clothing. And the aroma of her perfume made him want to lift her into his arms and climb the stairs to her bedroom. Not a spec of horse smell on her.

"How am I going to keep my mind on the play with you wearing this?"

She chuckled. "I can change if it bothers you."

He shook his head. "Don't do that. This is fabulous." What he didn't say was these new outfits revealed curves he didn't know existed on her and they were doing a number on his libido.

"You sure?"

"Baby, if I were any more positive we'd spend the evening here."

"Then I guess we better go," she said. Noelle had cautioned her not to wear her serviceable jacket, but it was cool in the city at night.

Honey, Drake will keep you warm, trust me. Noelle had said.

And like a simpleton, she wore a shawl with her slacks and top. With an obvious V, the top was a little more revealing than Jasmine was accustomed to. Noelle assured her it was just right.

Drake pulled off his jacket and put it in the

backseat before he got in behind the wheel. He turned the heat up and soon Jasmine was roasting so much she had to take the shawl off.

Jasmine glanced at him. He was sweating over there. She shook her head and reached over to turn the heat down.

"Hot?" he asked.

"You certainly are."

He chuckled. "Just didn't want you to strangle yourself with that shawl."

They were traveling against the traffic. The aroma of Jasmine's perfume floated in the air.

"Did you get a chance to catch up on your rest?"

"Shopping with Noelle? Please. She should be a professional shopper."

"Two days of shopping?"

"Can you believe it?"

They started out at a Mongolian restaurant in Chinatown. "It's not much for atmosphere, but the food here is delicious."

It was a create your own stir-fry where guests chose their own ingredients from a variety of meats, vegetables, salads, sauces and spices. The food was prepared by a master griller on a huge seven-foot grill. They chose their selections and handed the bowl to the chef to be cooked.

"This is delicious," Jasmine said once they were seated at their table. "I'm going to have to check out the restaurants in this city."

"I'll be happy to take you anytime you want to go," Drake said.

"You're so smooth. Always were. You always know the right thing to say."

"You don't think I'm for real?"

Jasmine shrugged. "I'm not touching that one."

"I'm wounded." But there was a mischievous twinkle in his eyes. Jasmine's heart skipped a beat. He was good, one of Steven's better friends.

"Have you heard from Steven lately?" Jasmine asked.

"He called not too long ago. Wondered how you were."

She scoffed. "I'm sure he's worried about me."

Drake merely shrugged. "Are you happy working here?"

Jasmine thought a moment. "Yes. I love what I do."

"Were you one of those kids who took wounded animals home to heal?"

"No. My mom wouldn't let me. She was always afraid of me catching rabies or some other disease.

I sneaked some in and cared for them anyway, but one of my steps always told."

"Annoying."

"What about you? Did your parents let you bring wounded animals home?"

"Actually, no. My mother would run both of us away if I so much as thought of bringing a stray animal in the house."

Jasmine laughed. "How did two misfits end up as vets?"

"Beats me. So are you going to let your children bring home wounded animals?"

"I'll patch them up. We'll probably end up with a houseful of them. Just like you and your dog. I already know you're a pushover. How is Hugs?"

"Very well."

"So tell me, how many children do you want? As if our careers would let us have time for them."

For a second, Drake's fork hovered in the air. "I haven't thought about children. My career isn't quite where it needs to be yet. Getting the office straightened out is the immediate goal," he said. "To ensure we aren't working these crazy hours forever. We're having an office meeting Sunday afternoon. We don't have anyone to handle things while I'm away. I'm grateful Floyd pitches in. I'm all for working hard, but we need a life, too."

"I don't know what having a life means anymore. It seems I've been working on one project or another since college. I spent every summer away. What about you?"

"I usually spent summers home. I worked at the National Zoo and in some vet offices," he said. "Why did you spend your summers away from home?" he asked, although he thought he already knew.

"I couldn't wait to leave home, and once I did, I never wanted to go back. So I'd comb the career center for summer internships that would take me away. And I found them. Every summer. Which is probably the reason my mother is bugging me now. But you never told me how many children you wanted."

"How many do you want?"

"Probably two. I want to have enough time to spend with them. I want to make sure they'll know they're wanted. And the man I marry will be totally committed to them. They won't be like me."

"Like you in what way?"

"My mother's husband didn't give me a second glance after they divorced. After all, I'm not his real daughter. I don't want this 'step' business.

I'm not going to impose all that drama on my children."

Drake's heart sank. But he tried to rally anyway. "Not all stepchildren feel that way. There are wonderful stepparents out there who treat their stepchildren well. Who provide as much for them as they provide for their own children. You can't paint all people with the same brush."

"I think this generation of people are more selfish. It's not the way it was in my grandparents' day. People did what they had to do to survive. They were willing to give more."

"Some are today, too. I couldn't have asked for better parents. And Noelle's parents loved her."

"You were lucky and so was Noelle." Her mouth twisted wryly. "This conversation is depressing me."

"Then we'll change it."

"The food is delicious."

Drake gazed at her as if a thousand thoughts were flowing through his mind. "I thought you'd like it."

While watching the play, Drake's mind wasn't on the show at all. He was thinking of Jasmine and the fact that she would not settle with a man who wasn't the father of her children. It was a broken record playing over and over in his mind. Let's face it. Her fears were valid for anyone with her background.

Perhaps one day he'd settle with a woman who already had children or go the artificial insemination route. He wasn't ready for marriage, but it bothered him that if he were to get entangled with Jasmine there was no future.

Right now, she was the only woman on his mind.

What was he agonizing about? He had the hots for Jasmine, but he wasn't ready to propose to her. They may never get to that point.

Drake tried to focus on the play, but he couldn't. Jasmine laughed and he laughed, too, although he didn't have a clue what he was laughing about. At least she was enjoying it. After the week she'd had, with work and rushing to finish her house, she needed to unwind.

Drake placed an arm around her shoulder. With a smile on her face, she glanced at him, but immediately refocused on the play.

Drake watched Jasmine from the corner of his eye. With her eyes closed, she leaned her head against the headrest as if she was completely relaxed. He was anything but. It was late and the sultry tunes playing on the R&B station didn't help matters. The sexual tension in the car was so thick you could slice it. He could tell himself to distance himself from Jasmine now, while it wasn't too late. But in his gut he knew it already was.

Drake pulled into her driveway and let out a long breath. Jasmine was watching him.

"Invite me inside, Jasmine."

Jasmine's mouth was dry as dust. She wet her lips with a flick of her tongue.

Drake groaned.

"Won't you come in?" she asked.

They barely shut the door behind them when Drake pulled her into his arms. Need, hot and intense, had built from the tiny fire of their last kiss, slowly driving him insane. He stroked her hair and then, holding her shoulders in his hands, he kissed her cheek, strung sweet kisses along her shoulders and neck before his mouth covered hers hungrily. He gathered her into his arms, pressing her body close to his.

Shivers of desire raced through Jasmine. She wrapped her arms around him, eager to meet his desire. She felt the hardness of him pressed against her thigh.

Drake felt a slight tremble and knew she wanted him every bit as much as he wanted her. He wasn't satisfied with sweet kisses anymore, even though the taste of her lips took his breath away.

Drake swallowed hard. He felt this was some pivotal moment in his life. As important as any of the thresholds he'd climbed. If he told her the truth, she'd be lost to him forever. But he had to make things clear. He took her face in his hands.

"I can't offer you a future, Jasmine," he said. "Or anything beyond what we have right now. But I want you." He caressed the side of her face. "I've wanted to take you to bed…"

Jasmine pressed her fingers against his lips. "I'm not asking for your future. Just the here and now."

Her vision blurred as his head moved closer to hers. Then he was kissing her again. And then he was holding her in his arms with her own arms wrapped tightly around him, feeling he held all that was important in his world close to his heart.

Jasmine's breath caught in her throat. She was astonished at the sense of need she felt. She'd dreamed of this, but had never felt this intense need and desire. Taking his hand, she led him upstairs.

Drake barely saw the beautifully decorated room, a feminine room, as feminine as the new

Jasmine. Or the candles and pillows. He flicked on the light. He wanted to see every inch of her beautiful skin.

He eased his hands beneath her blouse to touch her silky brown skin. "Your perfume is driving me crazy. *You're* driving me crazy."

She smiled shyly. "Is that all?"

"You're a vixen. This part of you is new. But I like it."

He gently pulled off her blouse and unhooked her bra, easing the straps down her arms before it fell to the floor. His hands sought her breasts and nipples before he kissed her there, drawing deep moans from her throat. Her hands began to roam over his body until he kissed her passionately and their tongues dueled like loving combatants.

"You taste delicious," he said as he strung delicate kisses to her cheek, her neck and her chest.

Jasmine melted like warm chocolate under his deft touch. She felt as if he'd lit a fire in her body. She burned with need.

She stroked the strong lines of his back, his biceps. She stroked the muscles in his arms. The term *velvet steel* came to mind. It seemed pretty fanciful to her. She usually didn't think in fanciful terms.

"The better to wrestle with the animals."

"Hmm," she said. His clean, citrus scent was driving her wild.

Cool air brushed her nipples. His tongue swirled around them bringing them to a peak and she moaned again.

"Like that?"

"Love it," she said as she eased her hands beneath his shirt and felt the solid wall of his chest. She brushed her fingers through the sprinkling of hair. She realized she'd never seen his chest before and she wanted to. But then he pressed against her breasts and the mixture of hair and skin and strength aroused her to an explosive level.

Drake felt like he was tasting heaven. He inhaled a sharp breath, trying to slow his need to take care of hers.

He unzipped her slacks and slid them off her hips along with her panties. He leaned back and gazed at the lovely view.

He feasted on her with his eyes. She gazed at him with a shyness that belied the barracuda in the office. He liked this softer side of her as much as he liked the strong vixen.

He urged her on the bed, and trailed kisses down to her stomach, her thighs. He teased her intimate secrets.

Her hands and lips on his body drove him crazy. He wanted this to be special for her—their first time together.

Her sweet moans steered him on. He kissed every part of her body, leaving no area untouched.

He reached for a condom and slid it on. Then it hit him. She couldn't get pregnant. For a moment he stared at her.

She tilted her head to the side in question. The luminous glow of need was on her face and in her eyes. He couldn't stop now. He'd think about problems tomorrow. There had to be a way for them to deal with this. He should have told her the truth. But right now he wanted—no *needed*— her too much.

Slowly he entered her and her body clenched around him. She was tight. For a moment he stopped and stared at her.

"It's been a while," she said around a moan.

Judging by her tightness, it had been a long while. She wasn't a virgin, but she wasn't very experienced, either.

Tenderly, he kissed her and felt her hands gripping his back. Her hips reached up to meet him.

He grabbed her hips and plunged deeply into her. "Am I hurting you?"

"No, no." She moaned against his lips.

He kissed her while filling her body with his own, time and time again. The pleasure was pure and explosive.

They moved in rhythm until they were both fulfilled and cried out in ecstasy.

Drake gathered Jasmine tightly in his arms and kissed her gently before he left the bed and went into the bathroom to find a washcloth. Now he took the time to notice the room was beautifully decorated. More feminine than he expected from Jasmine. He wondered if this was Noelle's touch. He didn't care.

Drake ran the water until it was warm and wet the washcloth. He brought it back and gently wiped her. After taking the cloth to the bathroom he got into bed and gathered her in his arms. He kissed her softly on the brow.

"You want to talk about it?" he asked.

"No."

"There hasn't been that many, has there?"

"No."

"You're so beautiful," he said. "Thank you for this gift."

She reached up to caress his face, then kissed him on the lips and settled back in his arms.

Almost asleep, she wrapped her arms around him. Completely content, Drake dozed off, too.

Half an hour later, he said, "I have to go."

Jasmine opened her eyes. "So soon?"

"Can't leave Hugs alone all night."

She tightened her arms around his neck, kissed him, then loosened her grip. "Okay."

Drake caressed the hair around Jasmine's face. "Jasmine, come to dinner with me Sunday. At my parents'. My mom is a mean cook."

Jasmine started to turn away, but he stopped the movement.

Puzzled by her reaction, Drake asked. "What's wrong? I want them to meet you."

"I don't know if we're ready for that. We're moving so fast."

Drake frowned. "I don't want you to be a secret."

"I just don't know where this is leading. You made it clear up front you didn't want any serious entanglements."

"I want entanglements. I just can't promise… I want you to meet my family."

Jasmine inhaled deeply. "Does it mean that much to you?" When he nodded, she asked, "What time?"

Chapter 7

When Jasmine burst into the office the next morning, Drake was already there with two cups of coffee.

"Want one?"

"Sure. The parking lot at the coffeehouse was full. You must have gotten there early." Their hands touched when he handed her the coffee and as much as Jasmine wanted "work as usual," the very air around her seemed electrified. To cover her unease, she sipped the coffee and picked up her schedule. "I must still be on leisure time."

"I got there during a lull."

"When? At five?" She was chattering nonsense to cover her morning-after anxiety.

"Close," he said, not displaying any of the apprehension that was tearing her insides up.

"I was thinking last night."

"About us?"

She smiled, losing her balance. "That, too. But I was wondering why Mr. Avery didn't sell the practice. It has to be a lot for him to handle in addition to the horse farm. He's always traveling to races and they have a thriving breeding program. So why does he need this?"

"Probably hasn't gotten around to selling yet, but it was his son's business. They say you shouldn't make any major changes the first year."

"I just hope he holds on for now. It's a bad time for changes."

"It will shoot my plans all to hell."

They were the only ones there and Drake set his cup down, gathered her into his arms and turned her to face him. Their lips almost touched before Jasmine brought a hand to his chest and pushed lightly.

"We can't do this in the office," she cautioned.

"Our only witnesses can't tell, now can they?"

"Drake, if we get in the habit, someone could walk in on us. I don't want to push that personal-professional barrier. There's already enough tension here."

"Okay." He stepped back, putting distance between them. "Then I'll see you tonight."

Jasmine nodded.

"In case I forgot to tell you, the house looked lovely. Maybe we can light the candles next time, or a fire in the fireplace."

"Maybe."

"So, since you aren't on call this weekend, will you go horseback riding with me? Maybe a picnic or something. Colin invited us."

"You're not going to believe this, but I don't know how to ride."

"You're kidding."

"I've never ridden a horse," she said as she shook her head from side to side.

"Well, then. I'll have to give you riding lessons. For christ's sake, you work with them every day."

"Yes, well…I didn't grow up around horses."

"But in college?"

"Never got around to the lessons."

Drake shook his head before his eyes searched her in frustration. "After the lessons, do you think we can ditch the newly-engaged for a while?"

"I'm sure you're crafty enough to find a way. I'll leave the details in your hands."

"Thank you." There was something lazily seductive in his look. "I'll take care of the business immediately."

A car door slammed and a minute later, Jeff came in with an armful of books, dropping two on the floor when he tried to close the door.

"I'll get the door for you," Drake said quickly, closing the door as Jasmine helped him with his things.

"Follow me to the office. I want to talk to you. Oh." He sniffed the air. "Coffee's already made. Thank God." Frowning, he turned and preceded them down a short hallway. Drake and Jasmine glanced at each other with puzzled frowns and followed him.

Jeff stacked his things on the desk and after pulling off his blazer and hanging it up, he made a beeline for the coffeepot and poured himself a cup before returning to flop into a chair. Drake and Jasmine moved some things aside so they could sit. They heard the outside door open again.

"Oh, good. This way I don't have to go through this twice." Jasmine heard footsteps and then Ponce appeared in the doorway.

"I've got some bad news, so we're going to have to make some decisions quickly," he said. "You remember Floyd's father died a few months ago. The will is being executed and he'll get a nice little inheritance. Someone bought out his horse farm a year ago. He'd run into some problems. His father had initially funded him. But refused to loan him more money to keep the practice going. It was in a rural area and he needed more vets. He didn't earn enough from cows and pigs to make it work. But he had suppliers, equipment and enough clients to get a good offer. He's not great at management."

"So why the hell did Mackenzie offer him a job here?" Ponce asked.

"Floyd's father asked him to. When George Avery was going through some financial difficulties, Floyd's father gave him a low-interest loan. Gave him some breathing room to pay off debts and get on his feet again. Mackenzie felt he owed him."

"Jesus."

"This meeting has to be about more than this information dump," Drake said.

"Floyd told me last night that he was going to offer to buy the practice from George and that he'll have to lower the wages after the huge payout."

A flicker of apprehension pounded in Jasmine's temples. She couldn't afford a cut in salary.

Ponce slammed a fist against the wall. "I'm out of here. I looked at a couple of places while I was on vacation. I'll give you four weeks, then I'm gone," he said.

Jeff stood. "Ponce, I'm going to talk to George today. Wait until then to make your decision. I've set up an appointment. There has to be something we can work out. George won't let his son's practice be run into the ground. I know he won't. If you can just hold on."

"Floyd has never carried his load," Ponce said.

"Maybe not as a large-animal vet, but he's a salesman. He brings business here," Drake said. "You can't discount his value. He grew up in horse country. He knows these people."

"What good does that do when we need bodies out there tending to horses. That's where our bread and butter is. Sorry, Drake, but we're not all working with dogs and cats. Quite frankly, small-animal fees don't keep the bills paid."

"He doesn't just get business for small animals," Drake countered. "He's brought in hefty equestrian accounts. You can't deny that."

"Maybe the focus should be on how all of us

can make this work," Jasmine added. Sometimes Ponce's attitude was a stretch. "I thought the purpose of bringing on Drake was to take care of all animal needs. To have a more rounded practice. At least I thought that was what Mackenzie wanted. Drake's carrying his weight here."

"Excuse me, but just because you two are dating doesn't mean…"

"Keep the arguments centered on business," Jeff warned. "You're not the only vet here, Ponce."

Ponce waved his arms. "I've got to get to work. This conversation is pointless anyway. George owes Floyd's father. He won't offer us anything. Heck, we can't afford to buy him out. It'll take a miracle for me to stay on. You got any miracles in your accounts?"

"You're just too hotheaded," Jeff said.

"I don't know about the rest of you, but if I were you, I'd start sending out résumés."

This wasn't what Jasmine wanted to hear. But Ponce was on a rant. The three of them would have to work together to come up with some solution.

She had huge loans from veterinary school, so did Drake, but their salaries were more than enough to handle that—if the practice continued as it was.

"We can discuss a game plan Sunday night."

"We're already overworked because Floyd doesn't do his share of the work. What do you think is going to happen when he takes over? He'll be playing golf and still not doing his share of the work. See you later." Ponce stomped down the hall and slammed out of the door.

"Well," Jeff said, wiping his brow, "that went well." He sighed heavily. "Look, I've been here twelve years. Mackenzie gave me this job when I was desperate. I learned as I went along, and apprenticed at other operations to learn how to run this office. Quite frankly, I like it here. I don't want to have to send out résumés, so if any of you have ideas, please be forthcoming."

"Ponce is right, we do need more vets. Would you like me to go with you to meet with Mr. Avery?" Drake asked.

"Yes. I know your schedule's pretty tight today, but maybe during lunch we can go over some things."

"Unfortunately, I'm working late. But I agree, we do need another vet," Jasmine said.

"Part of that is because Floyd is bringing so much business our way. But Ponce doesn't understand that."

Jasmine stood and glanced at her watch. "Or refuses to recognize Floyd's value."

Jeff shuffled his papers. "There's a lot Ponce doesn't understand."

Jasmine's brows were creased as she left the office. Drake wanted to do something to ease her worry. When the receptionists and techs arrived, there was nothing he could do. Besides, she didn't want to let everyone in the office know their personal business. Ponce had already lent credence to her worry.

Drake, who had the usual routine office visits of injections, physicals and injuries, was assuring an older woman that her beloved poodle was in good health. It was almost two in the afternoon and he was laughing about something the tech had said while he took a ten-minute breather outside to eat his sandwich. The tech took a cigarette break several yards away. He leaned against a maple tree while Drake sat at a picnic table. The sandwich was almost to his mouth when it struck him how much he enjoyed his work and the scenery.

The mountains to the west were a burst of beauty. Jeff had planted some flowers, and when he was stressed he'd piddle around in the flowerbeds. He had been doing that often lately. Azaleas and begonias were bursting with color. Even the rental house lent a gorgeous mountain view. Yet the mountains held back the worst of the winter weather.

Drake had been so set on his goal of moving close to D.C., he'd failed to realize how much this practice meant to him. Anyway, he was close enough to drive in for entertainment. What was an hour's drive in this area? If the growth rate continued to climb, the D.C. metro area would soon spread to West Virginia, anyway.

Drake quickly finished his sandwich and guzzled down a bottle of water. In a few minutes, he'd have to meet with Jeff to discuss their strategy with Mr. Avery.

It would certainly make things easier if the older man knew Jasmine was his granddaughter.

That evening, after Drake got home, Steven called him. He had just gotten out of the shower and was dressing to go to Jasmine's place.

The meeting with Mr. Avery had been hopeful. He didn't make promises, but at least he'd listened patiently to their offer.

"What's happening, man?" Steven said. "I've

been calling and leaving messages that you don't return, by the way. Are you ignoring me?"

"Just busy. Plus, I've already told you that I'm not going to reveal anything about Jasmine."

"I just want to know how things are going."

"Okay, except she's working too hard. But I hope we can remedy that."

"Has she introduced herself to the old man yet?"

"No. He had a nephew that tried to pass a wannabe actress off as Mackenzie's long-lost daughter. Jasmine says she thinks he'll think she's trying to pull a fast one if she reveals her true identity. Like a DNA test wouldn't prove it. But I think the real reason she's holding back is because of her mother. I think her mother feels threatened. She keeps warning Jasmine not to impose herself on him."

Steven sighed. "I think she should tell him."

"It's Jasmine's decision. I'm sure she'll tell him in time—if she's here long enough."

"What are you talking about? I'm hoping she'll settle down there, at least for a few years."

"We might all be looking for jobs."

"Why?" Steven asked.

Drake told him about the offer to sell the practice.

"Is that a bad thing?"

"I don't know. Floyd has good people skills, but you need more than that to run a successful vet office."

"Mr. Avery won't sell it if he knows Jasmine is his granddaughter. He'd want to keep her there. It's only fair."

"She wouldn't do that and I wouldn't ask her to."

"I know you wanted to move closer to the city."

"I like it here, but that's neither here nor there."

Steven clicked his tongue. "You and Jasmine are stubborn."

"It's our lives," Drake said, wishing he hadn't mentioned the potential sale.

"That's true. I can only do so much. The past is the past."

"It doesn't help that her father bowed out of her life."

"I called him. Told him how well Jasmine's doing. Asked when he called her last."

"I think you're going overboard on this guilt thing. Now you're getting too intrusive. You don't know what effect talking to her father after all these years will have on her. A lot is going on right now."

"I don't know. He said he'd call. I gave him her number. I don't know if it will help."

"What good is connecting with her going to do now? She's grown. It's going to take a lot to build that bridge after he's neglected her for so long. Besides, she's in Virginia and he's in California. She doesn't need him as much as she needed him while she was growing up."

"You're right. Anyway, take care. I'm going to try to get down to Virginia before too long."

That was what Drake was afraid of.

Slowly he hung up. He was concerned about the effect the impending trip would have on Jasmine, but he was also concerned about other things that directly impacted them both. He and Jasmine had made love. The best loving he'd ever had, and lovemaking that he'd initiated. So where the heck did they go from there? Especially with his secret. He wasn't comfortable enough to talk to her about it.

Suddenly Drake felt years older. Especially since Jasmine wouldn't entertain the idea of adopting or using a sperm donor.

But he wasn't ready to let her go and give up. Besides, if he were to believe his grandmother, life wasn't in his hands anyway. She believed there was a plan for everyone. Life sure as heck didn't go the way of *your* plans—but was guided by God.

So right now his gut was telling him to stick with Jasmine. He was in the company of a woman where the relationship felt right. And he wasn't going to let a little thing—actually, with her it was a freaking mountain—stand in the way.

Jasmine quickly showered and lit the candles downstairs. She was rushing trying to get everything done before Drake arrived.

She'd just finished setting everything to rights when he knocked on the door. She smoothed a hand down her side, pressed one to her galloping stomach and inhaled a deep breath before she marched across the room to open the door. Man and dog stood as a pair on her doorstep.

"Okay if Hugs comes in?"

"Sure." She bent to pet the dog and it sidled up against her. "Hi, Hugs. You're a sweetie." She glanced at Drake as he perused the room. "Don't keep me in suspense. How did the meeting go?"

"We gave him our pitch. He said he'd get back to us. He hasn't decided whether he'll actually sell yet. So it's anybody's guess which way he goes."

"Oh, well, I'd hoped for more than that."

"I think the big problem is we're going to lose Ponce either way."

"Well, I know a large-animal vet who spent a couple of years in Africa who wants to return to the States. He's sending out applications. I met him my first year in vet school. It's an option if Ponce decides to leave."

"We'll need at least two vets if Ponce leaves," Drake said.

Jasmine nodded.

"I ordered us something for supper. Are you hungry?" Jasmine asked.

He closed the distance between them. "Hungry for you."

Jasmine's laugh was half desire and half playfulness. Her stomach somersaulted. Maybe they should at least eat first. "You're insatiable."

"And don't you forget it," he said as he nibbled on her neck.

Heat stole over Jasmine's body. Her legs felt rubbery and leaden. This new relationship was different and as intoxicating as the most potent drug. His lips moved to her cheek eliciting a groan. "I...umm, what about dinner?"

"It'll keep. I won't." He slid a tongue along her collarbone. His hands stroked her breasts.

Jasmine melted like warm butter in his arms. She slid a hand along his skin enjoying the strength of his shoulders as muscles flexed with his movements.

His fingers tangled in her hair as he kissed her passionately. His hands sought her breasts and nipples causing a deep moan to escape Jasmine's throat.

"It feels so good to be with you," he whispered between kisses he planted gently on her breasts.

Just the sound of his voice was enough to make her go up in smoke. She felt as if she'd turned into a stranger.

He gently eased her down on the thick rug Noelle had placed in front of the fireplace. A brace of candles glowed within. The light flickered across his skin as his fingers danced across her body.

He pulled her blouse over her head and unhooked her bra, stringing kisses along the way.

Barely able to catch her breath in the storm of desire rocking her, Jasmine's hands roamed his body, catching his sweater and tugging it over his head.

Drake tried, he tried to contain his emotions to pleasure her completely. But it was damn near impossible as her mouth danced across his chest.

Catching both her jeans and panties in his

hand, he dragged them both down her lovely hips and legs. Then he pulled back and gazed at her. The heat from the candlelight was nothing like the heat flowing in his blood.

He leaned over her, kissed her thighs, felt the muscles tense and relax under his mouth. He kissed and tasted her until she was in a sexual frenzy.

Jasmine dragged his pants off him. Her eyes devoured the muscles of his torso, the thick patch of hair on his chest and lower.

They touched, caressed, kissed and stoked each other's bodies to a glowing flame so intense it nearly undid them both.

He grabbed his pants and searched for a condom, dropping it on Jasmine's stomach. She opened the package, taking it out, sliding it gently on him while stroking him at the same time. His moan of intense desire nearly undid her.

Drake positioned himself on top of Jasmine and gave them both what they wanted. Every inch of his long, hard penis penetrated her completely. Jasmine's hips thrust forward to receive every inch of him. For a moment he was still, every muscle in his body straining until Jasmine's gaze met his.

Then he began to move. They moved in cadence

like a choreographed dance. Each giving and taking as the tension built…and built…until they
exploded, like a volcano blowing its top.

Afterward, they collapsed in each other's arms.

Drake kissed Jasmine's brow and held her
tightly. "You are so beautiful."

Jasmine smoothed his brow. "You must need
glasses."

"It's true."

The flickering candlelight still burned around
the room. As he eased himself beside her, he wondered how he'd ever give her up.

Hugs sidled over and licked Jasmine's nose.
She laughed, breaking into Drake's thoughts.

"She must be hungry. As hungry as I am," she
said.

Drake loosened his grip and Jasmine eased
out of his arms. He felt alone without her. "I'll be
right back," she said. With her backside presenting
him a fantastic view, she picked up her clothing and
headed to the stairs. There was untold pleasure in
watching a naked woman march across the floor.
When she was completely out of sight, Drake
hauled himself up and dragged on his clothes.

Hugs quickly settled into their space in front of
the fireplace.

"You're cramping my style, buddy. You're on your own next time."

Hugs merely yawned and rested her head on her paws.

Drake had spent the night at Jasmine's place. But now, the next evening, his words haunted her. He'd said he could not promise more than what they shared now. There was no future for them. After spending the night in his embrace Jasmine couldn't help but wonder why. He didn't fit the image of a man who only wanted to toy with women. He was so much more—deep and caring. So what was preventing him from a serious relationship? What secrets was he harboring?

It was around seven and Jasmine was less than five minutes from the office. She felt content in a way that was so foreign she was unsure of how to handle the emotion or to trust it.

Jasmine rotated her shoulders. Though the hours she'd worked that day weren't as long as on some days, the strain on her body was worse. She'd had to deal with another thrashing colicky horse. She certainly could have used the tech that day, but he'd worked with Floyd.

Jasmine chuckled. Noelle had asked her to join

a local gym with her. With the workout she got, she hardly needed a gym. Still, she considered it. But when would she have time to use it?

She pulled into the office parking lot and parked in a space beside Drake's truck. These late-night sexual marathons were taking a toll on her. She massaged the back of her neck, grabbed up her purse and left the truck. For a moment, she stood there taking in the warm breeze.

"How is Noelle's shopping going?" Drake came over scaring the dickens out of her. Jasmine pressed a hand to her heart.

"Make some noise when you're there," she said. "You scared the daylights out of me."

"Hard day?"

"And then some. The furniture arrived. Noelle called an hour ago and said she had everything in place. She complained that I wasn't much help. No telling what the place looks like. I hope it's not all frilly." Jasmine shrugged. "When I emphasized that, she told me to let her make the decisions since I complained so much about the shopping. I guess she didn't like my input."

Drake chuckled and leaned beside her against the truck so close his arm touched hers. Her skin tingled. Then Hugs snuggled up to her and absently Jasmine reached out and rubbed her. Hugs rested her head against Jasmine's leg.

"Your dog is a heartbreaker."

"She has moves," Drake said with a smile. "So should I pick up dinner on my way home?"

"Why don't I cook? I took chicken breasts out to thaw."

"You can cook?" They'd had delivery the night before.

"Of course. Mama made sure of that. Just because I don't like to cook doesn't mean that I can't."

"You're on. Do I have time to stop by home and shower?"

"Sure, and bring Hugs with you. I'm sure I can scrounge up something for her."

Chapter 8

It was around fifty degrees when they started out on their ride at eight on Saturday. Leila had packed a picnic-basket breakfast and the scent was wafting out. They rode along the pasture of hills and valleys toward the lake.

Jasmine felt as if the huge horse was going to throw her any second. There was a world of difference between working with one with a stable full of people on hand and while standing on your own two feet than in trusting one to carry you along without dumping you on your behind.

Drake and Colin talked for a moment until Drake rode up to Jasmine. The darn horse was side stepping.

"Relax and hold on to the reins. Let her know who's boss."

"*She* is. I must be insane. To think I could have spent a perfectly good day sleeping in."

"Then you wouldn't be with me." The low timbre of his voice sent ribbons of desire through Jasmine.

Mr. Avery approached them, grabbing Jasmine's attention. "Maybe you should come by here and let me give you riding lessons, Jasmine. A large-animal vet should know how."

"Thank you, but I'm not going to be riding that often."

"We'll see," he said, looking concerned. "You all take care of her. Colin, maybe you and Drake should ride on either side. Better still, why don't we saddle up an old nag? Be easier for her to handle."

"She'll be okay, George," Colin said. "Quit babying her."

The ride to the lake was a transit through hell with the horse going in the direction it wanted to until the four of them rode side-by-side. By the time they neared the lake, Jasmine had a cramp in her hand from gripping the reins so tightly. She worked with horses every day and it didn't bother her. This felt different.

Two picnic tables were near the lake. Also a gazebo and a river-stone fireplace someone had already lit.

"Who made the fire?" Jasmine asked, gingerly dismounting and rubbing her hands together. She linked the horse's reins around a post and walked on rubbery legs toward the flames. It was chilly that morning and the dew was still heavy.

"I did. I know you women hate the cold." Colin rubbed Noelle's arms.

"I certainly do," Noelle said as she began to unpack the picnic basket. "I don't know why you guys wanted to eat out here when we could have eaten in a nice warm kitchen. We could have waited for the temperature to rise to go horseback riding."

"Haven't you ever hiked in the cold? It's fun," Colin said. "You've still got too much city in you."

"You're insane," Noelle said.

"Yeah, but you love me."

When Colin wrapped his arms around Noelle, it almost brought tears to Jasmine's eyes.

"Hey. You aren't going to cry on me, are you?" Drake murmured from beside her.

"Of course not." Jasmine moved to the picnic table and started to take items out of the basket.

"I could eat a bear," Drake said.

"Let's hope one doesn't smell this food or we're in trouble."

"We aren't that far out. Hey, you two. Enough of that. I'm hungry."

"Any more appointments today?" Mr. Avery asked later that afternoon.

Jasmine dusted her hands off. "This is it."

"Why don't you have dinner with us? Colin will be back here in an hour or so. Noelle's home but she'll come over by dinnertime. Girl doesn't like to cook."

"Thanks, but I just want to go home and clean up." She spread her arms. "I'm a mess."

Mr. Avery chuckled. "This is a horse farm, honey. We're used to messes. You can clean up at the house."

Jasmine wrinkled her nose. "I wouldn't go in anybody's house like this."

"We do all the time. I'm sure we can find something for you to wear. Just raid Noelle's closet. She won't mind. She always keeps extra clothes here. You two look to be about the same size." He motioned her toward the truck and Jasmine fell in step with him.

"It's isolated where she lives," he continued. "and I don't like the idea of her being there alone. She stays here sometimes to humor me."

Jasmine had skipped lunch. Her work was so physically taxing she could eat a cow, and she hated to wait until everyone arrived. But if she went home, she'd have to wait until she prepared something.

"Sure. I'll be right up." Suddenly she felt guilty. It wasn't like she and Drake had made plans, but he usually anticipated that they'd be doing something together. She'd call him. He'd emphasized there were no tomorrows with them. He wasn't her keeper, but it was a matter of courtesy. She knew he'd wait. She'd become dependent on seeing his face nearly every day.

Jasmine dialed his number. He was with a patient so she left a message.

By the time she sent the info over the Black-Berry to the office computer and drove to the house, Leila had already chosen an outfit for her.

"If you don't like this you can just go in there and choose something yourself," the older woman said.

"This is fine, thanks."

Leila seemed to be able to do a thousand things at once. "Did you see Burt at the stable?"

Jasmine wondered at the question. "Just for a few minutes."

Leila nodded. "You must be starving. I'll bring some snacks up while you're in the shower."

"I'll come down for them."

"Well, don't dawdle. I think George wants to talk to you. He's been acting strange the last couple of days. That man. There's always something going on. Never a boring moment."

Puzzled, Jasmine started to the bathroom.

"Just hand me those clothes and I'll wash them for you," Leila called out.

"Just give me a plastic bag to store them in and I'll wash them when I get home," Jasmine said.

"No need. I got a washer downstairs. Just hand 'em over."

Embarrassed, Jasmine quickly undressed and handed the grungy items to the woman. Obviously, Leila was accustomed to handling clothes where the wearer had wrestled in a stable.

In the shower, the warm water cascaded over her and the pleasingly scented soap smelled and felt heavenly. It had been a long week. Floyd was on call. This was supposed to be her first complete

weekend off since arriving in Virginia but she'd
had a call at Rocky Ledge Farm.

Sunday was already taken. Drake wanted her to
meet his family. Which meant that this dating business was getting more serious. A man didn't take
a woman to meet his family unless he was serious.
But he'd made it clear that things could only go
so far.

Drake was a puzzle. As kind as he was, he
kept his own inner battles close to his chest. For
the last couple of weeks, she'd either been at
work or with him. But now that she had time to
think she realized the relationship was onesided.
He knew her deepest desires and hurts. She only
knew his goals, but not what touched his core.
There was something definitely troubling him.
She sensed that much.

They needed to talk.

Jasmine rinsed off and turned the tap off before
she gathered up a towel to dry off with.

What luxury, she thought as she used the warm
fluffy towel to absorb the water from her now
clean skin.

Feeling pampered, Jasmine descended the
stairs. Mr. Avery came out of the library to meet

her. He was dressed in a jacket and gray slacks. Much more formal than she was.

"Join me in the den," he said. "It's a cool night so I lit the fire. It's nice and warm in there. And Leila brought in a snack."

Jasmine rubbed her hands together. "The fire and snacks sound wonderful."

In a gentlemanly manner, he held out his elbow. She linked her hand in the crook of his arm and he guided her into the study.

As they entered, Leila was setting platters of snacks on a table in the corner. And with one look at the cozy room, Jasmine was immediately enveloped in comfort. A warm glowing fire. Shelves and shelves of books. Comfortable seating. It was such a lovely room. She wanted to curl up and relax on the couch.

"Don't eat too much," Leila muttered. "I have dinner on the stove almost ready to serve."

"The snacks look delicious."

"Well, help yourself," Leila said before she left.

"I think I like this room best," Jasmine said. "Anyone could get lost in the comfort here."

"Feel free to come here anytime you like," Mr. Avery said, letting her arm go to pour her a glass of wine.

Jasmine's laugh had a nervous edge even to her own ears.

Mr. Avery handed her a plate and she piled on some of the snacks and began eating. "This hits the spot. Aren't you going to join me?"

"A spot of brandy, perhaps." After he poured himself the drink, he wandered over to a side table. "This is my son, Mackenzie. He was a large-animal vet, just like you."

"I know. A picture of him hangs in the office."

"His mother and I were very proud of him when he graduated with his veterinary degree. He could have majored in anything and I would have been satisfied, but it did my heart good that he loved horses the way I do."

"I'm sure he lived up to your expectations."

He picked up another picture and handed it to her. "This was his mother. She died ten years ago."

Jasmine set her plate on the table and took the picture of her grandmother. "She was very lovely," Jasmine said around the lump in her throat.

"Yes, she was."

Jasmine's stomach tied in knots. She needed to tell him the truth, even if he rejected her. The only way to do it was to just blurt it out.

"Mr. Avery," she said.

"Yes?"

"Your son, Mackenzie, was my donor father. I'm not here by chance. And I don't want anything from you, nor do I expect anything," she said quickly, remembering his nephew and the actress. "I came because I wanted to meet you. I wanted to know about Mackenzie."

He looked stunned. A flicker of apprehension coursed through Jasmine as he regarded her closely. Her mind was a crazy mixture of fear and hope, but the fear was overwhelming.

"It must have been the eyes and nose that made you look so familiar," he finally said. "Leila mentioned how familiar you looked every time she saw you. I don't know why I didn't recognize it from the beginning. Please, tell me about yourself. Did you always want to be a vet?"

Jasmine cleared her throat. Was he accepting her just like that? "From as far back as I can remember. I know lots of children want to be vets, and they outgrow the fantasy, but it was more than a childhood dream for me." Jasmine couldn't believe they were having this conversation.

"As it was for Mackenzie. I'm glad you're working in the practice he started. It's only right that his own flesh and blood follow in his footsteps. I can't tell you how happy I am to have you for a granddaughter. I don't want to step over my bounds, but I just can't contain my joy." He stopped. Took a deep breath. "When Mackenzie died I thought my life had ended, too. It was bad enough when my wife died, but at least I had Mackenzie. But without him, what was all this for? I'm an old man."

"Not that old." She smiled.

"Tell me about your family," he said.

She told him that her mother was the personnel manager for a large company in L.A., her stepdad was an accountant; and then she filled him in on her stepsiblings. "They will be visiting soon," she added.

"I'd love to meet them."

Jasmine knew that wouldn't go over well with her mother.

"Were you happy growing up?" Mr. Avery asked.

"Sure. There were always things to do. I liked the year-round nice weather, but I like it here, too. The snow should be nice."

"I'll remind you of that when you have to drive to your appointments through it."

Jasmine chuckled and began to relax as he continued asking her questions about her life.

"How did you find me?" he finally asked.

"Mackenzie left it so that I could contact him when I turned eighteen."

He regarded her a moment. "If Mackenzie had told me that he was going to be a donor when he was in veterinary school, I would have opposed it vehemently. But then I wouldn't have you and Noelle, would I? It was years after he married before they discovered his wife couldn't have children. It was a disappointment for both of them. For his mother and me, too. We always wanted grandchildren," he said. "But the Lord always works things out for the best. We don't always know His reasons for arranging our lives the way He does. I'm so happy you're here and I hope you will let me be a part of your life."

"You don't know me. How can you accept me—" she searched for words "—just like that?"

"You're my granddaughter. That's all I need to know."

All her life she had wanted the acceptance of a man. Her father, her stepfather, boyfriends. She was never good enough to keep them. And here, this relative stranger was accepting her without question. Jasmine's chest hurt. She couldn't breathe. She needed distance so she could think this through.

Darn it, she wanted to cry. She didn't want to fall for this man only for this to backfire in her face the way everything else had.

He looked at her expectantly. She didn't want to disappoint him.

"I don't know what to say," she finally said. "I never expected to even tell you, much less…"

"You don't have to say anything," he said quietly. "We'll take it one day at a time. I would like you to spend the rest of the weekend here. Noelle needs to know she has a sister. I want to tell her about you."

"She's been very good to me," Jasmine said.

"Can you spend the weekend?"

"Tonight I can. I actually have plans for tomorrow."

"Thank you. And Jasmine?"

"Yes?"

"Don't worry about the practice. Your job is safe."

"I've always earned my way with hard work. I don't expect or want any special privileges now," she said. "As a matter of fact, I don't want anyone to know I'm your granddaughter yet."

A flash of disappointment brushed across his face before he quickly contained it and smiled. "For now, let's just get to know each other," he said quietly.

* * *

An hour later Jasmine spoke to Drake on the phone. "I told Mr. Avery I'm his granddaughter."

"And how did he respond?" he asked.

"I can't believe it. He's really happy I'm his granddaughter."

"Anyone would be happy to have you for a granddaughter. You're a wonderful woman, Jasmine Brown."

She chuckled. "You're biased."

"You bet I am."

She was blissfully happy, fully alive. "It was a night of dreams," she told Drake. She relaxed on an overstuffed couch in the huge bedroom. It was all her childhood dreams come true.

"I'm glad for you," Drake said.

She missed him, really missed him. "How is Hugs?"

"All healed. I think she misses you—almost as much as I do."

Her heart leaped. "I miss you, too. I know this news is going to cause all kinds of friction in the office. Ponce will jump on it immediately. And so will Floyd, because it's going to affect Mr. Avery's decision about the practice. I don't want anyone to know I'm his granddaughter right away."

"Secrets have a way of revealing themselves," he responded after a moment.

"I mean it. I'll be very angry if word gets out."

"I won't say a word."

"Well, give Hugs a hug for me. What a play on words."

"What about me. I need one, too."

She made kissy sounds. This was not the usual Jasmine. She felt so giddy.

"Are we still on for Sunday?"

"Definitely."

"I'll see you soon."

They disconnected and Jasmine lay back against the couch cushion. She was so hungry and nervous before that she didn't take the time to appreciate her room. Decorated in green and burgundy, her suite was beautiful. Heavy drapes matching the bedspread covered the window. A zillion pillows rested on the bed. The room was larger than her two bedrooms put together. It had a green couch and floral chair. And a little writing desk occupied one corner. There was even a tiny refrigerator. Jasmine got up off the couch to inspect the contents. It had sodas, a bottle of white wine and bottled water.

Maybe she should put a small fridge in her

guest room and her mother wouldn't have to go downstairs during the night for a drink of water.

She was bone tired, but felt too energized to sleep. There was a knock at the door.

"It's me," Noelle called out, and Jasmine beckoned for her to enter.

"Here's a bathing suit. Let's have a swim. Or we can hang out in the whirlpool." She tossed it on the bed.

"Tonight?"

"No time like the present. It's early still."

"Okay."

Noelle sat on the bed. "Grandpa told me. I'm glad you're my sister. I liked you from the beginning," she said, watching Jasmine closely. "I understand why you didn't say anything. It's hard to do, isn't it?"

"Very."

"You have to meet my brother. He'll be here soon."

"I'm looking forward to it. Is he Mackenzie's son?"

"No. He's my dad's. It just happened when they stopped trying so hard."

Jasmine wondered if that had happened with

her father, although her mother swore his second wife got pregnant by another man.

Noelle headed to the door. "I'll meet you downstairs."

So much for sleep. Jasmine took the two-piece swimsuit into the bathroom to change. Noelle would understand what it felt like to be the product of artificial insemination. She knew how it felt for a father not to be a father.

Jasmine finished changing and joined Noelle.

"For me?" Drake asked when he picked Jasmine up. She placed a beautiful arrangement of flowers in the backseat.

"For your mother." He'd been so sweet to her. She took a rose out of the bunch and handed it to him with a kiss.

"May I have another one?" he said, drawing her close and deepening the kiss. When he drew away, he said, "I think we have an audience."

Sure enough, Jasmine glanced toward the house to see Mr. Avery and Leila standing at the window. She waved and got into the car.

They started down the long lane to the highway.

"I told my mom I was bringing a buddy," Drake said.

Jasmine chuckled, reaching out and stroked his thigh. "Is that what I am? Your buddy?"

He grabbed her hand, holding it in place. "You're going to cause an accident, woman. Get me all heated up. To answer your question, I would have had to field a thousand questions from my mom had I told her I was bringing you."

"We wouldn't want a thousand questions now, would we?" It did not escape her observation that he didn't name their relationship. But they had made love. Everyone didn't take lovemaking as seriously as she did. She wasn't going to put too much stock in their intimacy. She wasn't going to hope for a connection that he'd already told her would never happen. But her stomach churned with the thought of being his...

"What are we?" Jasmine asked.

"I'm going to get the questions anyway after they meet you. I haven't brought a woman home in years. So tonight they will call, one by one."

"You didn't answer my question."

"I don't know."

"Good friends and lovers?" Jasmine suggested.

"We're more than that. You're special. There's no one else in my life."

Jasmine had hoped for more, but it was better

than nothing. He turned the radio on and she settled back in her seat.

"Have your parents met Steven?" Jasmine asked.

"Yes. He visited a few times."

"What did they think of him?"

"That he's fun loving and it will be a while before he's ready to settle down. Steven can be a charmer."

Jasmine was a little apprehensive about meeting Drake's family. She'd asked her grandfather—he'd asked her if she'd eventually feel comfortable enough with him to call him *grandfather* and while she couldn't say the word out loud, it had a nice ring in her mind—if she could pick some flowers to take to Drake's mother. Their garden was impressive, with roses and God only knew how many other varieties. She wasn't into flowers so she couldn't name most of them. Not only had he complied, he'd gone to the garden and picked them for her himself. When she came down that morning, a huge bunch of flowers was on the table, a breathtaking arrangement.

An hour later they drove into a nice development that ended in a cul-de-sac. Drake pointed out a brick colonial with several cars parked out front. They found a parking space two houses down. It seemed the entire family was in attendance.

When Jasmine handed Mrs. Whitcomb the flowers the older woman exclaimed over them. "Welcome to our home, Jasmine. I hope you're hungry."

"Ravenous." Jasmine didn't bother saying the last thing a mother wanted to hear—that she hated to cook. Mothers wanted to know their sons would be well fed by the women they settled down with. Settled down? Where was she getting these thoughts?

After small talk in the backyard, the family gathered around the dining-room table. Drake's father said a prayer and everyone dug in. It was quite a feast with a roast, macaroni-and-cheese, kale, fried chicken, sweet-potato pone and much more. Friendly jabs volleyed back and forth around the table. The atmosphere was so different from what she'd experienced in California. After a while she began to relax. This is how a family should be, Jasmine thought.

After dinner, Jasmine helped Drake's sister with the cleanup over his mother's objections. When Jasmine pitched in, she came in to help, as well.

"I think you're a very nice young lady, Jasmine. Do you like it here?"

"It's a beautiful area," Jasmine said. "I like it very much."

"I was so glad to get Drake back home. He was in Vermont, you know, until the summer."

"Yes."

"You must miss your family."

"They're visiting soon."

"What a joy that must be for you."

Throughout the experience, Drake's sister and brother had teased and joked good-naturedly. This attachment was something she was never a part of at home. But Drake's family included her. And there were never any vicious attacks.

Maybe the estrangement between her and her stepsiblings was *her* doing. Maybe if she had re-acted differently, they would have reacted differently to her. But she didn't think so. They didn't attack each other the way they attacked her. Why did she even have to go there? Because her family would arrive soon.

Drake's family was warm and lively. It was everything she'd hoped for as a child.

Drake ambled in and his sister nudged him out. But before he left, he glanced at Jasmine. She gave him a reassuring smile before he threw up his hands in playful disgust and left.

"They always want to know our secrets," his sister said.

"He's worried about his young lady," his mother said. "We'll take good care of you."

"I can hold my own," Jasmine said.

"You most certainly can. You're always welcome back. We've really enjoyed having you."

Jasmine felt warm and happy.

An hour later, Drake and Jasmine were on their way to Middleburg.

"So did I feed you to the vultures?"

"You have a wonderful family. No wonder you wanted to move back."

He grasped her hand and kissed the back. "Yeah, I'm lucky."

"Of course, they do want you to settle down and marry."

Drake kissed her once more before he let her hand go. Had she made a faux pas? She'd promised from the beginning that she wouldn't put any restraints on him.

"Well, who wants to settle down so young anyway?" she added.

Drake still didn't respond, so the subject dropped. The silence was as loud as a thunder roll and Jasmine felt a dip of disappointment. Another mile passed by before Drake turned the radio on. Only the strains of music infiltrated the car. Nearly another five miles passed before Jasmine couldn't stand the silence any longer.

"Do you want to talk about what's bothering you?" she finally asked.

"Nothing."

"So you're allowed to delve into my psyche, but not vice versa?"

"It's not like that. I was just thinking about the meeting."

"Liar." Anger overwhelmed Jasmine.

He didn't respond. He just let the silence hover. But she felt betrayed. He wanted to know everything about her, but he wasn't willing to share.

"You're being so unfair, Drake."

"Jasmine, there's nothing to tell."

Jasmine stared out the passenger window, giving him silence. "So much for, 'You're special,'" she finally said.

Chapter 9

Later Sunday evening all the vets met at the office for a meeting. Although he wasn't that large, Dr. Floyd Parker was a barrel-chested man. Which was odd with the amount of physical activity he got.

Ponce leaned back in his chair with his hands behind his head, glaring at the ceiling.

Jeff, with his funny-looking tie, tried to take over the meeting, but Floyd marched up to the front as if it were his due.

"First I'd like to officially welcome Jasmine aboard. Unfortunately we couldn't do a formal welcome when she arrived because of the tight schedule."

Ponce made a crude noise with his mouth, but everyone ignored him.

"I was virtually working seven days a week. You've done a wonderful job of taking some of the pressure off all of us, Jasmine, and we're glad to have you.

"I'm sure all of you know I wanted to buy into the practice and I made George an offer," Floyd said. "I got my answer Friday. He won't sell. We need to assess where the practice goes from here. If he's going to maintain ownership, we need to figure out how this place can work for all of us. This is a thriving practice…"

"Whatever plans you make won't involve me," Ponce said. "I've accepted an offer in Pennsylvania."

Jeff scooted back his chair. "You promised to give us at least a month."

"This is my month's notice."

"I thought we had this worked out," Jeff complained. "This puts an enormous strain on Jasmine…"

"I think this meeting can work as an opportunity for us to come up with strategies to make this place work," Jasmine said. "It's obvious Ponce isn't happy here. I wish you good luck in your new assignment." Jasmine was tired of hearing his bitching. And she wasn't going to be used as the excuse for him to stay on. "We can hire a temp until we find a replacement and until the practice's future is decided."

"I just don't understand it," Floyd said. "We've built this practice into something grand."

"I'll tell you what's troubling me," Ponce pounced. "You don't do your job. You're so busy bullshitting you leave most of the work to Jasmine and me."

"That's not true," Floyd said, his face red with outrage. "I do my share of the work."

Ponce made another rude noise.

"That's enough," Drake cut into the bickering. "You're leaving, Ponce. What happens to this practice is no longer your concern. Floyd makes enormous contributions, not in the same way you, Jasmine, or I do, but a variety of skills are necessary to make this work."

"You're all as blind as bats. You're working in the twentieth century instead of the twenty-first. You deserve each other. Good riddance." Ponce hopped up, grabbed his jacket and slammed out of the office.

The silence left was ominous. Floyd eased into a seat. Clearly, Ponce's assessment had hit him hard.

"Don't take Ponce to heart. He's one of those dissatisfied people who likes to drag everyone onto his bandwagon. I'd still be struggling trying to get enough clients in the small-animal end to make this profitable had it not been for you, Floyd. Having you here has made my transition smooth and I appreciate your contribution." He patted Floyd on the shoulder.

Jeff sighed and stood. "This is the last thing we needed."

"He's drawing negative energy into the office. We'll survive without him," Jasmine said.

"I'm counting on it," Jeff said. "When I first talked to George, he seemed amenable to working out a deal. There was nothing definite, but he was listening. Now, I don't know what's going on in his mind."

"I think the first item on the agenda is to hire more vets," Jasmine said. No sense in wasting the entire meeting on an issue they could do nothing about. "We need to approach Mr. Avery with that fact. We have more clients than we can comfortably handle."

"We can't choose all of them fresh out of vet

school. Many of our animals are expensive thoroughbred horses. We need an experienced vet, even if he or she is only here on a part-time basis."

"Since Mackenzie died, we haven't been meeting regularly. I think we should to run ideas by each other," Floyd said. "I have some friends. I can let it be known we're looking for someone temporarily."

"Good. I'll do the same," Jasmine said. "I'll e-mail my friend who is ready to leave Africa."

They discussed other problems with some of the cases they were working with.

"I think that we're still severely understaffed," Drake said. "We could use another small-animal vet, as well as two large-animal vets. Our schedules are still rather hectic. I don't have a relief. And the large-animal vet practice is increasing."

"As you know, George Avery owns the practice. This morning after church services he mentioned our long hours and the possibility of hiring on more staff. He also mentioned Jasmine is his granddaughter." Floyd leveled his gaze on Jasmine. "As he's the owner, his desires carry weight."

She'd asked him not to tell anyone. "I want to make one thing clear. His owning the practice is not a consideration with me. I got this job on my own merit and I expect to continue working that way."

"I wish you had told me in the beginning," Jeff said.

"My paternity is a long story which I will not get into now. I had never planned to tell Mr. Avery I was his granddaughter, so there was no need to reveal that information to you. If my working here is going to present a problem, there are many opportunities out there."

"If you don't make it a problem it won't be one," Floyd said.

"The very fact that you mentioned it makes it a problem."

"Suffice it to say, Mr. Avery will be very upset if you leave the practice," Jeff said.

"And you?"

He gazed at his hands. "I've had no complaints from our clients."

"I've always pulled my own weight. The work is hard enough. I won't put myself in a position where I'll have to second-guess every move I make because of an issue that has nothing to do with my work."

Floyd nodded and went on to other business.

When the meeting ended, Floyd pulled her aside. Jeff and Drake were discussing something as she went outside with Floyd.

"I just wanted to tell you that I knew from the very beginning that Noelle was Mackenzie's daughter. We went to vet school together and he told me he was a donor for her mother. But he never knew if he had other children. In the end, not knowing really bothered him. And the absence of Noelle from his life hurt him, too. Of course, this all took place before he got married."

Jasmine nodded.

"He told me he left it so that any of his children could contact him if they wanted to when they turned eighteen, and that he hoped they would. I just want you to know he loved you."

"May I ask you a question?" Jasmine said.

"Sure."

"I understand why Mackenzie was a donor for Noelle. But I don't know why he did it for my mother."

"He hadn't planned to, but the people at the sperm back told him that they received very few black donors and there was a woman who desperately wanted a child." He touched Jasmine's hand. "He really loved you and wanted to meet you."

Tears sprang to Jasmine's eyes. "Thanks for telling me, Floyd."

He touched a hand to hers briefly, leaving Jasmine's heart splitting in two.

She'd come too late. She should have tried to contact Mackenzie earlier.

"I still can't believe the news got out," Jasmine said. "I didn't want that. I'd specifically asked Mr. Avery not to tell anyone."

"I told you, secrets have a way of escaping. He's proud of you. And happy. He just couldn't contain his joy."

"I just never expected this to happen," Jasmine said. "Poor Floyd."

"He doesn't deserve the rap Ponce gives him. If it wasn't for the fact you'd be working for two people, I'm glad to see Ponce go. He puts a pall over the entire practice."

"Maybe." But there wasn't a thing she could do about it. "I'll e-mail my friend tonight."

"I have a couple of contacts I can e-mail, too."

"Noelle's family is coming to town this week. Her brother and father at least. Mr. Avery invited us over for dinner."

"Are you sure you want me along?"

"I'm sure. And I have to prepare myself for the arrival of my own family. Every week Mom calls threatening me with their presence. I'd be much happier if it were just going to be her and Norman, as we'd originally planned."

"It won't be as bad as you think it will. I'll be with you."

"I don't know. There's still that connection between you and Steven."

Drake caressed the side of Jasmine's face. "I don't go to bed with Steven. I don't feel this way about Steven."

"What way?"

"That I want to hold on to you and never let you go."

He kissed her. It was sweet and erotic.

"Want to go to my place?" he asked softly against her lips.

"Sure. Just drop me by the Averys' first so I can get my truck. I'll follow you."

"Okay."

"I'm sure Hugs is waiting for you. You must feel really silly running around calling her Hugs."

"The name's growing on me."

They got into his truck. "I liked your family, by the way. They're really nice."

"They're okay. They like you."

He said it as if there was a problem with them liking her. As if he regretted taking her to meet them.

"What's wrong with you tonight?"

"Nothing."

Yeah, right.

Two days later, Jasmine was contemplating Drake and his obscure behavior when the doorbell rang. She answered to find Noelle, offering a basket of food.

"From Leila." Noelle flipped her sunglasses on top of her head.

"I'll have to thank her." Taking the basket from Noelle, Jasmine carried it to the kitchen. "Would you like to have dinner with me?"

"I've already eaten. The house looks nice."

"You should approve since you decorated."

"Trust me, I do. Doesn't it feel more like a home now?"

"Yes, it does. Thank you. My mother will thank you once she gets over the shock." They made themselves comfortable in the family room where Jasmine had added a couch.

"I know I came unannounced and you don't have time for visitors on weeknights, but I wanted to talk to you."

"Noelle, feel free to come anytime." Sisters didn't have to issue invitations.

"It's just there was no one I could talk to who understood what I was going through until now. It's hard for someone who knows their roots to understand why my biological roots are so important to me."

"Girl, I went through the same thing," Jasmine said, nodding.

"I think my mother more than my father felt a sense of betrayal when I said I wanted to meet Mackenzie."

"*My* mother laid on the guilt trip," Jasmine said, relieved that she could finally voice her frustrations. "And is she good at that."

Noelle chuckled.

"It must be a 101-course they develop at a young age," Jasmine said.

"Can you imagine yourself doing the things your mother does?"

"Are you kidding? Never."

"You realize our kids are going to talk about us like this when they're our age."

"I know. I can't imagine myself old. My mother always seemed old.

"Can I get you a cup of coffee or tea?" Jasmine asked.

"Sure, tea would be good. I'll help."

Jasmine was still a little nervous as she and Noelle went to the kitchen to make the tea.

"Noelle, I hope you don't think I tried to deceive you." Jasmine set the water on the stove to boil.

"It's difficult getting the courage to tell someone you don't know, someone you've never met, that you're related. I went through it, too, with Grandpa. So don't give it a second thought."

Jasmine nodded. She poured the tea into a china teapot her mother had given her along with a couple of delicate cups and saucers. She put everything on a tray and carried it back to the family room. She took the time to pour tea for both of them.

Noelle added a spoonful of sugar before she blew on the tea and sipped. "It's nice to have a sister. There had to be a reason we got along so well. From the very beginning our relationship wasn't like a regular friendship."

"I noticed."

"We are so opposite. We don't like any of the same things."

"I don't know. We don't know each other that well yet," Jasmine muttered.

"But we will. Granddad wants you to move into the family home."

"I have a year's lease on this place. Plus, I worked too hard for my freedom."

"Well, before long he'll probably bring you a dog like he did me."

"He'll take care of it, because I'm away most of the time. And that's about to get worse."

"Why?"

Jasmine explained that one of the vets was leaving for another practice.

"How awful."

Jasmine shrugged.

"Jasmine, I had a purpose for this visit. I'd like you to be the maid of honor in my wedding."

"But…but that's a position for a close friend. Someone you've been close to for years."

"Cindy will understand. She lives in Memphis. I hope we can vacation there sometime. I lived there after I graduated from college."

"I'm truly honored." Jasmine set her teacup down and hugged Noelle. She'd never been a maid of honor before. She wondered what duties she'd have to fulfill. Whatever they were, she would gladly do them.

Jasmine didn't make friends easily. To be accepted so unconditionally brought tears to her eyes.

Drake stood on Jasmine's doorstep with Hugs trying to edge her way inside. It occurred to Jasmine that he'd given so much, way above what was expected of him. And what had she offered him?

Jasmine moved aside and the dog trotted in and immediately took her position in front of the fireplace. "Drake..."

"What is it?" Drake asked coming inside, closing the door behind him.

"I just realized this relationship is very one-sided. Soon you're going to resent me because you'll feel you aren't getting very much out of it. It's unequal."

"So you can determine whether I'm getting my fifty-fifty cut out of this? That's ridiculous."

"It's not ridiculous. You don't share, Drake. And you expect me to share with you, to trust you."

"I try not to betray that trust."

"This conversation isn't about me sharing with you. It's about you trusting me enough to share with me."

"I don't have any problems right now. If I did, I'd tell you."

Jasmine was so frustrated she could hit him. She merely stared at the blank screen of the TV.

"I missed you."

"Don't say that. You'll say what you need to say to soften me up."

"Are we going on women's intuition here?"

"Don't play games with me."

Perturbed, Drake threw up his hands. "There's nothing to be concerned about. I'm not seeing anyone else. You're the only woman in my life. When would I have time to look at another woman, much less do anything about it? All my spare time is spent with you."

Jasmine stared at the ceiling. "This is not about another freaking woman, and you know it. I didn't believe it, but men really are from Mars."

Drake laughed.

Jasmine tossed a pillow at his thick head. Hugs jumped up to participate in the game. Drake flung the pillow aside and grabbed Jasmine, bringing her to the couch with him. Setting her on his lap, he held her snugly against him.

"I can't tell you how glad I am you put a couch in here."

Jasmine wasn't ready to give in. "It was your suggestion. You even picked it out."

"And this is the reason," he said, tilting her head back and kissing her before she could object.

As Jasmine gave herself up to the pleasure of his touch, she realized he hadn't answered her question. Drake had merely diverted her attention—and she'd let him.

She cautioned herself not to lose her heart to him. This was only temporary. Except when he kissed her, when he touched her, he devoured her as if he could never—even if he lived a thousand lifetimes—get enough.

Jasmine was in the stable finishing up an ultrasound when Noelle's father and brother came in. Noelle squealed. Her father opened his arms wide and she sailed into them.

"How's my girl?" a handsome older man said.

"Wonderful. I'm so glad you're here," Noelle said.

"What an understatement." He hugged her again before he let her go and she was enveloped into her brother's arms.

It was immediately obvious it didn't matter at all that she wasn't his biological daughter. In every way that counted he was her father. He couldn't take his eyes off her.

"I hope you're ready to be whipped on the golf course," Mr. Avery said.

Noelle's father focused on Mr. Avery. "I can't wait to show you who's in charge out there."

Mr. Avery laughed and the men shook hands.

"Jasmine, come over here. Franklin, I want you to meet my granddaughter, Jasmine Brown. Franklin Greenwood is Noelle's father, as I'm sure you've already determined. And this young man," he said, pointing to the younger image of the older man, "is her brother, Gregory."

Jasmine extended a hand. "Pleased to meet you."

"Likewise. Did you grow up in L.A.?"

"Yes. My family still lives there."

He regarded her closely, probably trying to pick out similar features to Noelle.

Jasmine was uncomfortable with the perusal, but he soon looked away and started a conversation with Mr. Avery. He still had an arm slung over Noelle's shoulder. Noelle engaged Jasmine and her brother in a conversation but didn't let go of her dad. Jasmine was jealous, but at the same time happy for Noelle.

"Casey is eager to see you, knucklehead," Noelle said to Gregory.

Gregory smiled. "I can't wait to see her."

"Are you all settled in?"

"We dropped our stuff off at your place before we came over."

"Leila's cooking your favorite tonight."

"I'm glad I don't have to depend on you for food." Noelle elbowed him in the ribs.

"Owww. Give me a break. You can't cook."

"I can, and you know it."

"Not like Mrs. Leila," he grumbled.

"So you're the doc," he said to Jasmine. "Do you have some horse pills for my sister here to calm her?"

Jasmine laughed. "I might. Nice meeting you. I have a few more appointments before I can call it a day."

"You're coming to dinner tonight, aren't you?" Mr. Avery asked.

"I'll try."

"Make sure you still bring Drake with you."

"Okay." She glanced at Mr. Greenwood. "Pleasure meeting you."

When Jasmine left, she couldn't help thinking that these people were family. She'd finally learned to stop comparing families to her own. No, hers wasn't perfect, but she wasn't there any longer.

She had moved on.

Jasmine climbed into the truck and pulled away. It took a lot of years for her to come to that point. She owed Drake a lot, even if he was still keeping secrets.

Jasmine was in a strange mood when she got home that afternoon. Ponce was working late, but Drake got off a little early. After her shower, she dressed more feminine than usual. She carefully applied makeup. Spritzed on delicate perfume and the aroma hovered in the air. She finally settled on a pair of earrings after trying several pairs. Then she combed her hair into a beguiling style.

She was done just before Drake arrived. Taking a deep breath, she opened the door to him.

"Wow. Am I at the right house?" The light in his eyes made her insides quiver.

Jasmine laughed a high-pitched sound. It seemed as if she was someone else, not plain, dowdy Jasmine.

Drake gathered her into his arms. "I hate to mess up your lipstick, but..." He kissed her. It was sensuous, delicious. He swiped his tongue along the curve of her lips. She opened her mouth to him like a rose opening its petals.

They stood there, hovered in the doorway. Time

had no meaning as they enjoyed the texture of the kiss and the sensations that sprouted from need and desire.

"Thank you," she said when they finally parted.

Frowning, he asked. "For what?"

"I've come a long way since I moved here. And you're responsible."

"I can't take credit for what I didn't do," Drake said. "You told Mr. Avery who you were."

"Don't ruin my gratitude, okay?" With her arms linked around his neck, she brought his lips to hers, putting an end to the debate.

"Do we really have to go?" he whispered against her lips. "Can't we stay here?" He gave her a wicked grin full of mischief. "I promise you, you won't be bored."

Jasmine moaned. "We have to go, but who says we have to leave this second?"

"Not me. Definitely not me." Drake urged her back and used his foot to shut the door. He pressed her against the wall, the length of his body pressing against her own.

Jasmine rubbed her hands up and down his chest.

Forty-five minutes later, they finally piled into the car and drove to the Averys'.

"We are definitely late," Jasmine said, flipping the mirror down and reapplying makeup.

"Don't blame me. I worked as quickly as I could."

Jasmine scoffed, finished up her makeup and turned down the visor.

Drake kept watching Jasmine. She looked content seated in the passenger seat.

It had hit him when his body hovered above hers in the throes of passion. He was in love with Jasmine. And it had nothing to do with sex.

He'd kept secrets that would blow their world apart once he revealed them to her. He had to tell her. But not tonight. And not tomorrow. He'd wait until after Jasmine's family left after their upcoming visit. They needed a buffer and he was it. He wanted to support Jasmine while they were there, and once he revealed he was incapable of giving her children, he knew their relationship would end.

He sighed deeply. This would not be easy for him.

"What's wrong?"

Drake wished he'd stifled his sigh. He reached over to gather Jasmine's hand in his, but she moved her hands out of reach.

"You're really pissing me off."

"I know. But don't be angry, Jasmine. I want you to enjoy the evening."

This time she was the one who sighed and gazed out the passenger window.

Chapter 10

"We're packed and ready to leave early tomorrow morning," Jasmine's mother said on the phone. "We should arrive around eleven in the morning your time, and we're renting a car from the airport. Should be twelve or one when we arrive at your house."

Wonderful, Jasmine thought. "Mom, I've reserved a room for you in D.C. that's right in the middle of all the tourist traps. The museums, theater, everything you love."

"You just cancel that room, because we're staying with you."

"Everyone?" Jasmine's voice squeaked.

"Sure. All your brothers and sister."

"I have a tiny two-bedroom house, for heaven's sake. It won't hold that many people."

"We're family. We'll make do. Did I tell you when your father and I first married we lived in this tiny one-bedroom apartment?"

"A million times." Jasmine rubbed her forehead. "Mom, this house can't possibly hold that many people."

"Yes, it can. Your brothers can sleep anywhere. And you and your sister can share a bed."

"I don't share my bed. And don't they have friends in D.C. they can stay with? They must have met someone in college."

"Jasmine, Jasmine," her mother tsked. "You haven't changed a bit. You're still being difficult. I thought you'd grown up some by now. Now, everyone has put their lives aside to visit you and I expect you to be on your best behavior. Do not ruin this vacation."

"There's nothing to do here. I work from sunup until late into the night. This is a busy time of year for me."

"We'll manage, dear. We don't expect you to

entertain us. At least we'll get to see you on the weekend and in the evenings."

Frustrated, Jasmine finally said goodbye and hung up. She could never outdebate her mother. Amanda Brown Pearson always…*always* had the last word. Jasmine should have learned that long ago.

Good thing she'd let Drake talk her into a hide-away sofa for the living room. And he'd taken the tiny refrigerator up to the spare room the day they went to dinner at the Averys'. It was already stocked and waiting for her mother and stepfather.

She could pull the bed out and her evil step-brothers could sleep there. She hoped they'd stay with Drake. Then she wouldn't have to see them.

She just couldn't get the dilemma with Drake out of her mind. What on earth was he hiding? He could scoff at her intuition all he wanted, but she knew something wasn't right.

The day her family came to town, Jasmine arranged her appointments so that she could be home around the time they arrived.

When she drove home, the rental car was already parked in the driveway. In a shot, her mother was out of the car and hauled her into her arms, her Coach purse hitting Jasmine in the back. Jasmine was taller than her mother's five and a half feet, but her mother still held on to her trim shape. She wore blue slacks with a matching jacket and a white silk blouse.

Amanda leaned back and held Jasmine at arm's length. "You've lost weight."

"I don't think so," Jasmine said, enveloped in her mother's familiar perfume. She couldn't help it. As much as she complained, she was very pleased to see her mother. And although she never thought to say it, darn it, she really missed her.

"You always ate like a bird," Amanda said. "Just look at you." She hauled Jasmine into her arms again before she let her go. There were actually tears in her eyes. Jasmine felt guilty for not going home more often. Maybe now that all her stepsiblings were moving out, she and her mother could spend more time together.

Norman came up behind her and awkwardly wrapped his thin arms around her, then stepped back and nodded. "You're looking healthy," he said. He fit the stereotype of an accountant perfectly. Bottle glasses, lanky and definitely a nerd. But her mother loved him.

"Thanks." The evil stepbrothers and sister were lined up behind them, but none of them tried to hug her. They were a somber group, as if Amanda had roped them into coming. Otherwise they probably wouldn't have made the effort. They disliked her every bit as much as she disliked them.

Jasmine wondered what her mother had threatened them with. They were adults. They didn't have to come, but her mother always tried to establish a bond between them. Needless to say, she was always unsuccessful.

Suddenly Steven broke from the pack and approached Jasmine. "How are you, Jasmine?"

"I'm fine," she replied cautiously.

"It's good to see you. You're looking well."

"Thank you." Steven had played too many tricks on her for her to believe he was being genuine.

Jasmine dug in to her purse and retrieved a key. "I have to get back to work. Sorry I can't see you settled in. The place is a little small."

"I told you we'll be fine here," her mother said as if she didn't feel the tension circling in the air.

"Yeah, we'll be fine," Steven said, shocking Jasmine.

"We're invited to dinner tonight at six," Jasmine

said after she'd recovered. "So be ready to leave a few minutes before."

"How nice."

Before Jasmine could get the house door open, a truck came roaring into her driveway. Seconds later, Drake bounded out of the truck and everyone went toward him. Steven was the first to reach him, laughing and holding out a hand as if it were a lifeline in a thousand-foot-deep snowdrift.

"Hey, man. Good to see you."

"Yeah, you, too," Drake said, clapping Steven on the arm. The other siblings spoke. Barbara hugged him and Jack shook his hand. Then Drake hugged Jasmine's mother and shook Norman's hand. Everyone was laughing as if given a reprieve from the fricking gallows.

It was easy to put Drake and Steven's friendship to the back of her mind when her family was in L.A., but with them here it was front and center. How would she and Drake fare as a couple in the midst of this other friendship? Would he feel pulled in half with her on one side and Steven on the other? She hadn't thought this through.

Maybe this was the reason he'd been holding back. Steven probably told him he was coming to town.

Suddenly Drake was beside her. He kissed her lightly on the lips and slung an arm around her shoulder, which blew her reasoning right out of the water.

"I was hoping I'd see you before you got away," he said.

She smiled, but she didn't feel any humor. "You're just in the nick of time. I was just leaving."

"Can you stay for lunch, Drake?" Amanda asked. "We stopped by the grocery store on our way here. I can whip up something quickly."

"Another time, maybe. My lunch break is up soon."

"Dinner, then."

"You're on. Need help with the luggage?" Drake asked.

"We've got that," Amanda said. "The quicker you get back to work the quicker we'll see you later."

Jasmine had the door open and Amanda walked through. "Your bedroom is upstairs to the right. There's a hideaway in the living room." She led the way upstairs with her mother on her heels. Noelle had fixed the room up prettily with pillows, candles, framed art and things for the dresser and tables.

"What a pretty room," Amanda said. "Just like being in a high-class bed-and-breakfast."

"I hope you like it. There's a small refrigerator in the corner so you won't have to run downstairs for a drink."

"I love it already. Your place looks like a home. I worried that you lived in some stark hovel, but this is so nice, Jasmine."

"There are some brochures in the bedside table. Things you might want to see and do while you're here."

Amanda waved a hand. "We're going to be here at least a week. Plenty of time for that."

Oh, God, no. How would she make it through an entire week? One day at a time. "I don't want you to cook on your first day, so I've already arranged to have a late lunch delivered." She heard someone coming up the stairs. It sounded like Norman's lumbering steps.

"Now, why did you go and do that? I could whip up something."

"You've got plenty of time to cook. I have to go."

Amanda gathered Jasmine in her arms again. "It's so good to see you, honey." Her mother's eyes were glassy again.

Jasmine hugged her awkwardly. "You, too, Mama."

And then Jasmine ran downstairs, passing Norman on the steps. Outside, Drake was talking to Steven. He looked up when the door slammed and Jasmine headed for her truck. He left Steven's side and Steven pulled luggage from the trunk of the rental car.

"What time will you be in tonight?" Drake asked.

"In time to take my family to dinner with the Averys. You're still coming, aren't you?"

"I'll be there."

"Good, good." She glanced at her watch. "I'm running behind."

"Not too late, I hope. I want to see you."

"We'll see."

"Okay." He pulled her close and kissed her, then he opened her door for her.

"I don't get to do this often. You always beat me to it."

Jasmine shook her head and climbed inside. The last thing on her mind was a silly door she opened a thousand times a day. Drake closed her door and she watched him march to his truck and start the motor. He pulled out behind her. Once they reached the major road, she went one direction and he the other, but not before he tooted his horn. She waved and pulled off.

Would they ever be on the same wavelength?

He'd already made it clear their relationship wasn't going to be a lasting one. But she felt comforted by his presence today. At least he was with her now. But Steven was here, too, and his actions confused her. After the tricks he'd played in the past, she didn't know what to think.

Her cell phone rang and after looking at the number on the display, she answered.

"How are you?" Drake asked.

"I'm fine."

"Are you sure? If you need me to, I can take a few minutes to be with you."

Even if she wasn't okay there wasn't a thing she could do about it. "I have to get to my next appointment."

"Jasmine, sometimes you have to take care of you." His voice was firm. "You can be a little late. You can't always time these things anyway."

"Ponce already thinks I'm getting special privileges." He was mumbling something the other day. She'd immediately put him in his place because she wasn't going to let anyone interfere with her work. "I have to be careful about doing anything to give him or anyone else a reason to complain or accuse me of getting special privileges."

"Forget about him. You have to deal with your emotional state."

Nobody had ever cared how she felt. She felt a catch in her throat. "Just knowing you're in my corner buoys me," she said softly. "Thanks for caring."

"Glad to be of service. I'm here if you need me. You know that, don't you?"

"Yes, I do. Thank you."

"Can't wait to get you in my arms again. The other night was fantastic."

Heat flowed through Jasmine and spiraled in every direction. She sighed, wishing she could be in his arms now.

"What was that?"

She sighed again. "I'll see you tonight."

She could tell herself a million times it wasn't good to depend on another person. That didn't keep her from falling for Drake—the most unlikely person she could have ever considered falling for.

Drake grabbed a sandwich on the run and drove back to the office. Floyd was finishing up with a patient when he went in. Drake tossed his wrapper in the trash and guzzled the last of the water in the bottle.

"Thanks for covering for me, Floyd."

"Anytime," Floyd said. "I'll be on my way. Have a few shots to give this afternoon. Also, we have a movie star who moved here recently. I looked in on her horse the other day. She has a couple of toy dogs. I gave her your card just in case she needed a local vet."

"Thanks, Floyd."

He named the actor who used to appear on soaps.

"She's still quite the looker." He wiggled his bushy eyebrows. "And she's single."

"Even better."

Floyd looked around to make sure they were alone. "So tell me, have you talked to Jasmine about your medical issues yet?"

Drake shook his head.

"Don't you think you should?"

"It's complicated."

"It always is until you talk about it. Then you wonder why you took so long."

"The timing isn't right," he said. "Her family's visiting right now."

"Excuses. I know one thing. You're not going to get anything solved keeping it to yourself. You have to share. And if the two of you put your heads together, you just might come up with a solution. Now, take a stallion for instance."

"You're not going to start with one of your horse analogies, are you?"

"If it works, it works."

"You know, I could have gone all day without hearing that."

Floyd patted him on the back and left. Floyd was right about one thing. If he expected things to go further with Jasmine—and he wanted it to—he had to tell her soon.

Dread sank deep into his gut. He did not want to ruffle the smooth waters of their relationship. One little ripple could send it spiraling in all directions. What he feared was that it would go in any direction except the one he wanted it to go in.

And now Jasmine's family was here. This was the worst possible time to talk to her when she was already so stressed out.

"Where are we having dinner?" Amanda asked as she climbed into the car.

Jasmine was beginning to regret accepting the offer. "At Mr. Avery's."

"Avery?" Amanda asked. "He wouldn't happen to be Mackenzie Avery's father by any chance, would he?"

"Yes."

"Why did you contact him when I explicitly asked you not to? I think it's insensitive of you to impose him on us. You know how I feel."

"It would have been rude to refuse his invitation. He wants to meet you."

Just the two of them were in her truck. The others were riding with Drake.

Amanda sat tight-lipped as they rode up the impressive lane. It was still light outside, and the flowers and oak trees showered the thriving estate.

"Well, I see he's wealthy enough, but money can't buy love, Jasmine."

"I know that, Mama. I don't want his money. That's not why I wanted to meet him, and you know it."

"When I went into that procedure all those years ago, I went with the knowledge that Mackenzie was giving up all rights to you and that's the way I wanted it."

"Mackenzie is dead," Jasmine said, tiredly. "He isn't fighting for any rights."

They stopped in front of the house. Jasmine was glad to escape the confines of the truck. Drake parked his next to her. He raised an eyebrow at her pinched lips, then glanced at her mother, whose lips were equally tightened.

He shook his head as everyone piled out of his car in a jovial mood.

Mr. Avery met them at the door. Noelle and her family were already present.

"Good evening," Mr. Avery said. "Welcome."

A round of introductions were made, but everything went downhill from there. It was apparent her mother did not appreciate the Averys' interference in Jasmine's life. It was as if she felt Jasmine would abandon her for the Averys.

As affable as her grandfather had been, Jasmine's mother was tight-lipped and barely cordial, creating a pall over dinner. The succulent dinner Leila had knocked herself out preparing could have been sawdust for all the enjoyment they attained.

Jasmine could not have been happier when dinner ended and they were ready to leave.

"Mrs. Pearson," her grandfather said, "I hope you visit us again before you return to California. You're always welcome at River Oaks."

Amanda nodded her head. "Thank you for dinner. It was delicious." And they all departed.

Back at the house, still tight-lipped, Amanda got ready for bed. Norman quickly got under the covers, out of the line of fire.

Jasmine stayed downstairs with Drake, making sure everyone had towels and whatever else they needed. The strain had given her a splitting headache.

Her stepbrothers and sister escaped to the family room to watch TV, while Drake and Jasmine sat in the kitchen.

"I'm going upstairs to make sure Mom and Norman are settled in okay." Reluctantly, Jasmine climbed the stairs to her mother's room. Amanda had changed into her nightgown and was rolling up her hair with quick angry movements. Norman was pretending he was asleep.

"Do you need anything, Mom?"

"Not a thing," she retorted.

Jasmine sighed. "Okay." She went to her room. Her mother followed her and closed the door behind her. Here we go again, Jasmine thought.

"It's as if you don't think I provided a good life for you."

"It has nothing to do with you."

"You don't know this man. You don't spend time with your own family, yet you go out of your way to be with him. You didn't even want us to come. And you want to toss us into some hotel more than an hour's drive away."

"Mama, you know how your stepchildren and I feel about each other. We can't be in the same room without wanting to stab each other. I don't understand why you brought them, why you didn't just come with Norman. You probably had to pay for their tickets in addition to threatening them."

"From the time your father and I divorced and I remarried, you haven't made any effort to become a part of the family and that's all I want."

"My stepsiblings and I aren't family. I don't know why we have to rehash my childhood every time we talk. Some people just don't mix. It's just the way life is."

"Yet you and this Noelle act as if you're long-lost sisters."

"We are. Like it or not, we share the same genetics."

"I don't want to talk about it anymore."

They were at an impasse. Jasmine knew her mother was hurt. But she didn't know what she could do to fix it. She wasn't going back to California. Not in a million years.

"I have to go see if everyone else is comfortable," Jasmine said, walking through the door to make her way downstairs.

Drake glanced at her. She was unaware he was still there.

They'd moved the coffee table aside in the living room and pulled out the bed. Jasmine got pillows from the closet.

When she went back upstairs, she noticed her stepsister hogging her bed and talking on her cell phone to someone.

Jasmine went back downstairs and outside with Drake.

"How are you holding up?" he asked.

"This is already the longest night of my life."

"Come on, let's go for a drive. Get you to relax."

"I have company. I can't just leave."

"They're family. Besides, Steven has my cell-phone number for emergencies."

Gratefully, Jasmine climbed into his truck. "I have to work tomorrow."

"It's still early."

Jasmine glanced at the digital-clock display. "Then why does it feel like I've been up for forty-eight hours?"

Drake inserted a CD into the player, turned the volume down low and gathered her hand in his.

Jasmine leaned her head against the headrest and closed her eyes, letting the flow of the music lull the tension out of her.

"Is that better?"

"Lots." Jasmine hadn't realized how quickly tension could dissipate. With her eyes closed, she'd almost nodded off when the car slowed and turned. The texture of the road changed and Jasmine opened her eyes. They were at Drake's place.

It was two-thirty in the morning when Jasmine returned home. The house was quiet. "If I'm lucky everyone will be in bed asleep, but with their bodies set to California time, I know they're still up," she said to Drake.

He walked her to the door, kissed her and gave her a comforting hug. Jasmine put the key in the lock, gathered her breath and opened the door. Most of the lights were out. Except the glare coming from under the door to the kitchen. Slowly she walked in that direction and opened the door.

Her mom was sitting at the table sipping on a cup of tea. Jasmine closed the door behind her. Then she made her way to the other end of the table, pulled out a chair and sat. All the stress that had drained off came roaring back like a tornado.

"You didn't have to leave your own home," her mother said.

"I just went for a drive."

"Until two?"

Jasmine let that ride. She was twenty-six. She supported herself. She wasn't going through that.

"I don't understand it, Jasmine. How could you accept that man who's never done a thing for you and you can't accept your own family?"

"I never got along with them, and you know it. You can't force a relationship between us. It didn't happen in all the years I lived in California. It isn't going to happen now. I wish you and Norman had come alone."

Her mother shook her head. She looked so desolate that Jasmine wished she could get along with her stepsiblings. But having them under her roof set her blood pressure soaring.

"Maybe I shouldn't have married Norman."

"Mom, none of this matters now. We're all grown. We've made our own places."

Her mother sipped her tea. "You haven't really been home since you finished high school. Every summer you went off on some project or another. Every summer—all summer. And then you took the little money you made to spend a week with a friend one place or another. As much as I asked you wouldn't come for more than a week." She rubbed her forehead with her hand. "I know I worked long hours when you were young. I had to to make a living. But I'd hoped that one day, maybe we could do things together. I'd save during the year so we could go on shopping sprees or visit museums, tour, something, anything together. To just…" Tears ran down her mother's face.

Jasmine felt tears slipping down her own cheeks. But she didn't go to her mother. She didn't know how to breach the chasm between them.

Jasmine plucked up a napkin from the holder Noelle had brought and wiped the tears from her face.

"There's a nice shopping center at Tysons. It seems like it has a thousand stores. I'll take you there after I get off work the day after tomorrow. Just you and me," Jasmine said. "And there are quaint little shops in Middleburg. You'll love going through them. We'll find time to do both."

There was such longing in her mother's eyes, Jasmine was forced to look away. In the silence they both sipped on their tea.

"Well, you better get to bed," her mother finally said. "You have work in the morning."

Chapter 11

When the alarm went off at six, Jasmine reached to turn it off and nearly fell on the floor. She was on the very edge of the mattress. Her feet fell to the ground and she pushed the off button. She glanced at the bed. Barbara was hugging the edge of the mattress on the other side.

So much for her mother's plans of them getting along.

Jasmine started to the bathroom and stopped. She smelled bacon and coffee. "Bacon?" she whispered. When she opened the door, she saw a faint light from downstairs. Only her mother would get up this time of morning to cook. She was on vacation, for heaven's sake.

Shaking her head, Jasmine headed to the bathroom and dressed in record time.

Her mother was washing a frying pan in the kitchen.

"Mama, why didn't you sleep in? I don't expect you to cook breakfast."

"Goodness, child. I'm used to getting up early. Besides, I doubt you cook before going to work. Thought it would be a nice treat for a change."

"It is, thanks. But I want you to get some rest, so sleep in for the rest of your stay."

"Just take your plate and sit before you're late for work." Her mother handed her a plate and a cup of coffee. Then she prepared a plate for herself and sat across from Jasmine. Their conversation from the evening before lingered in the air, but neither of them mentioned it. They talked about everything but.

"I prepared a plate for Drake," her mother said when Jasmine was ready to leave. "I'm sure he'll appreciate a nice breakfast, too."

"He would. Thanks Mama." Awkwardly, she hugged her mother and left.

In the office, her brain was still asleep. The coffee had pumped a little energy into her, but even caffeine didn't take the place of an extra three hours of sleep.

She poured herself her second cup. "I hope it's strong," she said to Drake.

"It's lethal. I take it things didn't go well when you returned home?"

"My mother was in the kitchen nursing a cup of tea when I got back. We had this little heart-to-heart. She wants to do things with me. Like shop," she said. "I'm not a shopper, but I promised her I'd take her to Tysons after work."

"She just wants to be with you, honey."

"Hmm, by the way, she sent along your breakfast." Jasmine handed him the plate she'd set on the countertop.

Drake groaned. "Remind me to kiss her," he said, taking the plate and removing the covering to glance at the contents.

"She likes you."

"I have that effect on mothers. So what are you going to do with everyone else while you and your mother shop?"

"I'm not going to do a thing with them. They will probably go to D.C. or something. I don't really care."

Drake looked at her in exasperation. "I'll entertain them so you can enjoy your evening with your mother."

"What a Good Samaritan you are."

"Steven wants us to get together anyway. What's a couple more tagging along?"

"Knock yourselves out." Jasmine gathered her things and headed to the truck. She was driving to her farthest point and would work her way in. Her cell phone rang. It was Mr. Avery.

"Jasmine, I was calling to make sure your family is okay and to see if you needed me to do anything."

"They're fine, thanks. And thank you for dinner last night."

"I got the impression your mother was upset," he said in a cautiously weary voice.

"Just family drama."

"Is there anything I can do, dear?"

"No, but thanks."

"Tomorrow night Noelle's father and I are playing poker. Do you think Norman would like to join us? I know it's short notice, but I wasn't comfortable inviting him last night."

Norman play poker? She could see him tallying the money and his accuracy would certainly be to the penny. But play? "I don't think he plays." And the men smoked cigars. She couldn't see Norman in that manly pursuit. He'd run outside coughing. More than likely he would spend the evening in the kitchen talking to Leila, keeping the older woman from her sleep.

"No big deal. We can teach him. Why don't I have Franklin call him?" Franklin was Noelle's father. Her mother didn't hold the animosity against him that she held against George Avery. For some reason Mr. Avery presented a threat.

"Sure." Let him try, although Jasmine knew he'd be unsuccessful. Her mother would disapprove and Norman liked to keep the waters calm.

Floyd called Drake later that afternoon to tell him he was visiting the movie star later on, and he wanted to know if Drake could stop by for an introduction. She had volunteered to help raise money for his orphaned animals. Drake readily agreed to go.

He had one more client. Marsha was bringing in one of her dogs for injections and a checkup before they left for a competition.

"Are they competing in the Westminster this year?"

"They certainly are, the dears," she said. Marsha loved dogs, and these were well-pampered ones.

"Just wanted you to know the fund-raising plans are going very well. The new movie star who moved to town has already offered to help out. Her face will certainly bring in the money," she said, raking her fingers through the dog's fur. "And we're getting volunteers organized, as well."

"Thanks, Marsha. I truly appreciate your efforts. I'm actually going to meet her later on today."

"Well, good! It just breaks my heart to see animals suffer. If my husband would allow it, I'd have a kennel of my own. But he doesn't share the same love for animals that I do."

"You're helping by arranging things."

Soon after Marsha left, Drake left for his visit to the movie star's place. The gate was closed when he arrived. He announced himself at the loudspeaker.

The massive iron gate opened and he drove up to an impressive home.

"Good evening, Dr. Whitcomb. Do you mind if I call you Drake?" she asked when she opened the door.

"I don't mind at all, ma'am," Drake said.

"What's this ma'am business. Please call me Katie, I insist." Katie was his mother's age. She'd dressed in expensive lounging pajamas that flowed smoothly on her beautifully sculptured body. Her face was slightly bruised, as if healing from plastic surgery.

"I'm here to talk to you about our vet practice..."

"Floyd has already done that," she said. "And he's convinced me you're an excellent vet. Why don't I introduce you to Biddy and Puddles?" She left for less than a minute and returned with two purebreds that came charging and barking into the room, coming to a quivering stop a couple of feet away.

They immediately sidled up to Drake. He cautiously reached out to pet them. They flipped over for him to rub their bellies.

Drake squatted to pet the dogs.

"I see you love animals as much as I do," she said.

"Yes, I do." Drake glanced up and resumed his position on the couch.

"I love animals and Marsha has told me you've taken on more than you can comfortably handle. I'm willing to make a donation, as well as participate in your fund-raising event. And since your land joins mine, let's see what we can do to develop a small zoo area where people can make a small donation to tour. I saw something like that in Florida."

"I like that idea," Drake said.

"It wasn't that much. We could build large enclosures so the animals could move around more freely."

The phone rang.

"What rotten timing," she said. "I'll be just a sec."

In a moment, she was back. "Floyd's on his way. He'll be here in a minute." Then she patted her hair. Was something going on with her and Floyd? Drake wondered.

The little fund-raising plan was going to work quite well, Drake thought.

"I don't know why you told Franklin you'd play cards," Amanda said to Norman. "You could go shopping with Jasmine and me."

Jasmine had showered and was dressing to take her mother shopping.

"I want you to have time alone with Jasmine," Norman said. They were in their bedroom.

"You don't play cards."

"I can learn. People from work invite me sometimes. It's time I learned to do some new things."

"I don't want anything to do with that man and his family. And I don't want you over there."

"You're going to make yourself sick. Just calm down, sweetheart. Now, don't badger Jasmine. Just go out and have a good time."

"But..."

"Try, sweetheart. I love you. Now, remember, no unpleasant topics. Pick out some nail polish, or clothes, or...whatever you women do." He seemed at a loss for words. "Drake picked up the others a half hour ago. I may as well play cards with the men."

"I don't know," Amanda said.

"Franklin will be here soon. I'm going to head downstairs. Do I match?"

"Of course you match. I packed all your clothes. Here, you may as well take the key in case you get back first."

There was a period of silence. They must be kissing, Jasmine thought. Then she heard Norman's footsteps on the stairs.

Good old Norman.

Jasmine finished dressing and opened her door. By the time she went downstairs, her mother was already in the family room and Norman was gone.

"I think we'll check out the shops near here Saturday," Jasmine said, "and go to Tysons' now."

Her mother gave a half smile.

"I'm so glad to get out of that house," Barbara Pearson said with a sour face.

"I'm sure the sentiments are mutual," Steven said. It surprised Drake that Steven spoke up for Jasmine. Right then and there, Drake wanted to drop Barbara off in the middle of a forest and let her find her own way home.

"I don't understand how you can even stand her, Drake."

"Maybe because she's the best thing that ever came into my life," Drake said with more feeling than he'd intended. But he meant every word.

"It's like that?" Steven asked.

Drake nodded. "I don't understand why you all came if you feel this way."

"*She* made us come," Jack Pearson said.

"She?"

"The Dragon Lady. Amanda," Barbara clarified.

"But you could have begged off. You're all grown. You could have found a million things to do. And Jasmine could have enjoyed the time with her mother and your father."

"Steven here has changed into Mother Teresa. And when Dragon Lady wants something, you follow the plan, or else."

"At twenty-two and twenty-four you two are grown," Drake repeated.

"When I was a kid, you could barely move without that woman dishing out punishment," Barbara said. "We'd lose our allowance, or she'd keep us trapped in that tired old house if we stepped out of line. She'd think of all kinds of punishments. Dad never punished us. But you don't cross *her.* And I need to move back home. Rent is expensive and my roommate ran out on me. I can't afford the place. So what could I do when she laid down the law but waste a week here?"

"I don't think you're going to be able to move back home. I heard her telling Dad she'd raised us and she wants them to spend some time alone," Jack said. "She's tired of us moving in and out. It's a shame, because I need a place, too. We've been paying the rent late, and they're kicking us out."

"Dad's an accountant," Steven said. "How often has he talked to you about managing money?"

Barbara's sigh was long and tired. "I'm still young. Clothes are expensive."

"Especially when you're buying designer brands," Jack said.

All Drake could do was shake his head.

"I don't know why he married her in the first place," Barbara finally said.

Steven turned around in the seat. "He's in love with her, guys."

Drake knew it had been bad for Jasmine, but he just now realized how bad, and for Amanda, too. His hand almost trembled with anger. With this background she'd never marry him. When Jasmine had witnessed how well Noelle got along with her father, he'd had a glimmer of hope that things could work out for him and Jasmine, but with this attitude...he just couldn't blame her.

And Jasmine had to sleep with this witch, Barbara, every night. Their presence was going to put a pall over Jasmine and Amanda's time together. Amanda desperately wanted to share this experience with her daughter.

"The nightlife in D.C. is much more lively than out here," Drake offered. "Why don't you get a hotel there for the rest of your stay? I'll even spring for it."

"God, anyplace would be more active than this boring burg," Barbara said. "I'm about to die from boredom."

Steven shifted in his seat. "We had a talk before we left L.A. We're going to try to mend fences with Jasmine."

"No." Drake shook his head adamantly. "You can mend fences if you want to, Steve, but I want them out of her house."

"What's up with you? You sleep with the woman and now you've gone crazy?" Barbara said. "Don't worry. I have a friend in D.C. who wants me to visit. I'll just give her a call."

"You do that."

"I've got someplace to stay, too," Jack said.

"Mind if I hang out with you?" Steven asked.

"Sure, man."

Drake had lost every bit of energy he possessed. He might have told Jasmine all they could count on was what they shared right now, but he never believed it, not really in his heart—until now.

Well, if he couldn't marry her, the least he could do was rid her of the nest of vultures. They were the worst kind of human beings. Jasmine was too decent to have to waste time on them.

"Norman's glasses are going to fog up when he sees you wearing that outfit," Jasmine said with a mischievous smile.

"Oh, girl." Her mother blushed as she modeled a classically sensual lounging outfit from an upscale store. She glanced at the tag for the third time, as if she needed an excuse to purchase it. "Well, it is on sale."

"Splurge for once. All of us are grown and on our own. It's time you took care of you."

"I think Barbara and Jack want to move back in."

"You're kidding!"

"I told Norman I don't mind lending them money if I have to, but I want my house to myself. I knew the responsibility I was taking on with raising his kids when we married. But I never expected to do most of it alone. We need some time together. I need a break."

"Of course you do. I have a little extra, do you need some help?"

"Oh, no. We're fine. Norman was always good with money, you know that."

"If he taught me nothing else, he taught me how to handle money," Jasmine said, remembering the long, boring sessions. But she'd listened. Better than his own children.

"I wasn't going to get anything for myself." Her mother was looking at the price tag again.

"No fair," Jasmine said. "You forced me to buy

several outfits. As a matter of fact, since I moved here, I've bought more clothes than I did in college."

"Well, to repeat your own words, it's time you did something nice for you. Now, let's get manicures."

"You get a manicure," Jasmine said, looking at her nails. "I'm a vet, Mom. The animals don't care. Besides, I have to wash my hands a million times a day. It would be a waste of money."

"You're a woman, and don't you forget that," Amanda said in her stern voice. "Drake would love to see you all dolled up. Is it serious between you two?"

"I think so." With her family underfoot, she had little time to delve into her relationship with Drake. She knew he was holding back, but she didn't know what his big secret was. Just that it had to be serious, and that worried her. She knew he wouldn't divulge his secret until he was ready. What could it be? "He's special."

"And he thinks the world of you."

That was just it. Jasmine knew he cared for her, so what was going on?"

"We'll get manicures, and then have dinner. How does that sound?"

"Perfect."

Amanda disappeared into the changing room.

Jasmine never expected to enjoy the outing with her mother so much. She had been dreading it, actually. She was so glad she'd agreed. In the past, she never took the time to really appreciate her mother. Still in her early fifties, Amanda Pearson was a lovely woman.

"Hand me your clothes, Mom," Jasmine said. "I'll get them on the hanger while you dress."

"Okay. Here they are."

When Jasmine got the outfit, she took it to the cashier and paid for it. She wanted to do something special for her mother.

A minute after the cashier handed her the shopping bag, Amanda came out of the changing room. "Where's the outfit, honey? I'll pay for it and we can leave. I'm getting hungry."

Jasmine held up the bag. "Right here."

"You paid for it?"

Jasmine leaned close to her mother and kissed her on the cheek and gave her a one-arm hug. "A gift from me."

"Oh, thank you, sweetheart." Amanda dabbed at her eyes. "But I didn't want you spending your hard-earned money on me. You've done so much.

The bedroom is so special. And all the extra touches you did to make our stay wonderful."

"You've done that my entire life." Jasmine hugged her mother again. "Let's go."

When Jasmine and her mother finally made it home around midnight, Drake, Steve and Norman were downstairs watching TV and munching on snacks Leila had sent home. Drake noticed everyone stiffened as if hit with a stun gun when the key hit the lock, even him.

"Well, we had a wonderful evening," Amanda said, bustling into the door. The women left a stack of packages in the foyer.

The next reaction was as if a group of collective balloons had been deflated. Each male smiled at Amanda's jovial mood.

Norman stood. "Looks like you bought out the store."

"Just a few things. Jasmine bought me the loveliest outfit. How was your evening, dear?"

"Wonderful. Franklin's wife came to town today. He asked if maybe the four of us would like to go sightseeing in D.C. tomorrow. I told him I'd get back to him after I talked to you. Do you have plans for tomorrow, sweetie?"

"No, but..."

"Oh, Mom, that's a wonderful idea," Jasmine said.

Amanda's face scrunched up. "I don't know these people."

"They're friendly, honey. Jasmine's here all alone. I think it's a good idea to get to know some of her neighbors."

"They live in California like we do."

"Their daughter lives here," Norman said in his usual calm and convincing manner, squashing her arguments one at a time. "She and Jasmine are friends."

"But what would we do with the kids?"

"Jack and Barbara went to visit friends in D.C.," Steven said. "And I'm going to spend the night with Drake. He's convinced me to hang out at the office with him tomorrow. I get to nurse his menagerie of homeless animals."

"Oh, well..."

"It's all settled," Drake said, before Amanda could come up with another excuse.

"Franklin said he'll be up late tonight, so I'll just take these packages upstairs and give him a ring." Norman took all the packages from the hallway and disappeared upstairs.

Amanda glanced around as if her world had turned on its axis and she'd been thrown off course. "I just don't understand why everyone's leaving."

"Don't worry about it, Mom. I'm sure they're bored stiff hanging around my place. This way I don't have to worry about you being at loose ends while I work."

"You know me. I can always find something useful to do."

"Got plenty of food here," Drake said. "Anybody hungry?"

"Oh, we ate," Jasmine murmured, rubbing her stomach, and sat on the couch beside Drake.

"Well, I'm going to sort these packages out," Amanda said, heading to the stairs. "Some of them are Jasmine's."

Drake stood, too. "Want to walk me out while Steven packs his things?" he asked Jasmine.

"Sure." They walked outside. "You want to tell me what's going on?"

"I don't know how you put up with those twits all these years. I spent a few hours with them and was ready to throw them off the mountain."

"Yeah, well. What did they do?"

"It's just their whole attitude. Steven is better. I think he's matured. But his sister and brother…"

"I, for one, am glad they're gone. I'm going to change the linen on my bed and sleep very well tonight."

Drake leaned against the column. "Looks like you and your mother had a great time."

"We did. I'm so glad we did this."

Drake dragged her into his arms, tugged his fingers through her hair, drawing her head back and kissed her deeply. "I miss you."

With her arms linked around his neck, her face against his chest she breathed deeply. She felt the soothing beat of his heart. "Oh, I miss you, too."

Chapter 12

It was around noon the next day when Jasmine's cell phone rang. "Look behind you," Drake said when she answered.

Jasmine peered into her rearview mirror. Sure enough, Drake was close behind her.

"There's a path about a mile up on the left. Pull into it."

"All right." It was a rarely used stretch of land the Averys owned. The road was rutted with potholes and overgrown with weeds. Thick stands of trees blocked out the midday sun.

Jasmine hastily parked and rushed back to Drake. He held the back door open.

"What's going on?" Jasmine asked.

"Come here, woman." He hefted her into the seat, climbed in after her and shut the door.

"I can't believe you." Jasmine laughed when he started kissing her neck and unbuttoning her blouse.

"I'm desperate. Your family's cramping my style."

When he tugged her blouse off and unhooked her bra, light spilled on her beautiful brown breasts. "God, you're gorgeous."

He suckled on a nipple, and Jasmine's smile turned into a groan.

"Just thinking about you drives me crazy. I didn't get a wink of sleep last night."

"Neither did I," Jasmine breathed. The feel of his warm breath against her breast gave her such intense pleasure. She tugged his jeans open and gathered him in her hand.

He swept his hands along her body. She stroked him until he was begging for release.

She found herself flat on her back.

"We're going to be arrested," she said around a moan as he slid on a condom.

"I'll be a happy man," he said, just as he plunged

deeply into her. Her hips rose up to meet him thrust after thrust, demanding more, their breaths panting with a need too long unsatisfied. The windows steamed up and springs groaned as they came to completion, their voices ringing out in the car.

Drake slumped against Jasmine as he crushed her against him. As her heartbeat decreased, the cool air brushed across her skin.

"I can get used to this midday treat," he said.

"Umm," was all Jasmine could manage. Minutes later she urged him up. "I have to make it to my next appointment," she said.

"What are your plans for tonight?" Drake asked, zipping up his pants.

Jasmine sat up, thankful they kept a supply of wipes in the truck. She grabbed her clothes and dressed.

"Mom called. They're going to the Kennedy Center. They'll be back late. What about you?"

"Too bad, I have Steven."

"How is he working out at the clinic?"

"Okay. He's spending the day in the barn with the animals. Doing chores I haven't had a chance to do. I plan to take him bowling with the guys tonight. You can come along with us."

"With a bunch of guys? No thanks. I'm going to bed early. You all have fun."

Jasmine kissed him, then left the car. She felt energized and naughty. And ready to take on the rest of the day.

When Jasmine made it back to the office that evening, all the energy had drained out of her. That's what she got for burning the midnight oil only to be up before five in the morning. She couldn't wait to get home to bed. She'd just make a quick trip inside before heading home.

And if she were lucky, she'd have a few minutes with Drake.

Steven was coming from the barn looking grungy and as if he'd worked the longest day of his life.

"Jasmine, can I have a word with you?"

Eager to get going, she asked. "What's up?"

"I just want to apologize for the way we acted as kids. I'm sorry we didn't make more of an effort to get along with you." Ill at ease, he jammed his hands into his pockets and stared at her as if he expected her to attack him, but was equally determined to see this through.

Jasmine nodded. She respected him for the effort. It was more than his sister or brother attempted to do. It was a little too late, but she thought of her mother's efforts and decided to try to meet him halfway.

"It was a long time ago," she said.

"Not really. There's still that barrier between us. And I know it's not going to be easy to bridge the gap, but I am sorry and I am thoroughly ashamed at how we behaved."

"Thanks, Steven."

"This has been on my mind for a long time. Which is the reason I asked Drake to see if he could get you on at Avery's Vet. You like it here, don't you?" he asked hopefully.

"Very much."

"I knew this would work out for you when I asked Drake to check out your donor father."

"You asked Drake what?" Jasmine was stunned.

"I thought you needed that connection."

Steven gazed at her for a moment longer before he patted her on the arm and hastily returned to the barn.

Jasmine started inside, and then changed her mind. But before she could leave, Drake came outside the building, his face wreathed in smiles. "Jasmine?"

When she took too long to respond, he approached her.

"What's wrong?" His voice was full of concern, and that innocent tone annoyed the heck out of her.

"Why didn't you tell me Steven asked you to search for Mackenzie?" Jasmine asked.

"Steven asked me not to. He wanted to atone for the past, but given your past he didn't know how to reach you."

"Please tell me that you've kept the conversations between us confidential."

"Of course I have. I wouldn't betray you. You mean too much to me."

Jasmine nodded. "Steven and I have made some progress and I'm grateful. But change doesn't occur overnight. It will take time for me to trust him. I may never trust him completely, but I'll try," she said. "My knee-jerk reaction is to protect myself from him. At this point, I have to consciously make myself relax in his company. As much as I want to, I can't forget sixteen years with just a snap of the fingers. Although, I admit, asking you to find my father was a kind gesture. I still need some time to deal with all this. I'll talk to you a little later." Jasmine quickly walked to her truck and drove off.

* * *

Jasmine went in early the next morning, long before Drake made his appearance.

She started at the Avery farm, where her grandfather came out to see her.

"How are your parents enjoying their visit?" he asked.

"Very well," she said. "Thank you for inviting Norman to the poker game. He really enjoyed it."

"Good. I'd like to invite your family to a barbecue late Saturday afternoon, since they're leaving Sunday. Noelle's parents are leaving around the same time."

"I don't think my mother will come," she told him bluntly.

"Franklin and his wife would really like to see them again before they leave. And so would I." At Jasmine's pause, he said. "I want to impress upon your mother that I'm not a threat. I just want to get to know you. I want to be a grandfather to you. It doesn't take anything away from her."

"That's the last thing you can say to her."

"Then I won't. I just don't want to cause you undue stress and I know the barrier between us bothers you."

"Some things just can't be fixed," Jasmine said. "But I'll ask them."

"I haven't seen much of you since they arrived. I hope we can start those riding lessons soon after they leave."

"I'm looking forward to them."

"Make sure you invite Drake, too."

"I will."

"I have a few things I'd like to give you when your parents leave," he said. "I have picture albums, and some of your grandmother's things. I also want you to become more involved with the farm. I know you're busy right now, but it's part of your heritage and your inheritance."

Jasmine shook her head. "Mr. Avery…"

"We won't discuss it now. We have plenty of time to iron all this out." He gazed into her eyes. "You aren't getting enough sleep."

"I'm fine."

But she wasn't fine. Too many things were going on all at once. She should be used to that by now. But since Drake had come on the scene things had been so much better.

That evening when Jasmine made it home, Norman was in the kitchen drinking a glass of juice. Drake hadn't called her all day. And she hadn't seen him. Her day just didn't seem complete without seeing him.

"I'm glad I finally caught you alone," Norman said, jerking her attention back to him.

"Did you want to discuss something with me?"

"I wanted to make sure you have your finances in order. In a small business like this, sometimes owners neglect things like adequate retirement and insurance. Those are necessary requirements these days. Not a luxury." He lowered himself onto a kitchen chair and wrapped his hand around the glass. "The younger you are when you start saving for your retirement, the better. Less money grows to larger sums than if you begin in your later years."

"This practice has both."

"You're sure you have adequate health insurance?"

"I'll give you my paperwork and you can check it out." If it was one thing Norman did and did well it was drill the principles of finances into them.

Norman nodded. "That's a good idea. Maybe when you come home we can take a trip to your favorite ice-cream shop. Your mother misses having you around."

"We'll do that." Jasmine reached out and

touched Norman's hand. His gaze jerked to hers. "I do miss you, Norman. You were always so good to me. Thank you."

Norman cleared his throat and pointed toward the window. "Looks like your young man has arrived." Norman had never been comfortable dealing with emotions.

Jasmine glanced through the window and, sure enough, Drake's truck was coming to a stop in front of her house.

Drake spent a few minutes with her parents before he asked, "Jasmine, can you get away for a little while?"

"Sure."

She got into the passenger side of Drake's truck and he jumped in on the other side, started the motor and drove away from the curb.

"Where are we going?" Jasmine asked.

"A quiet place to talk."

She turned on the radio to fill in the silence. The quiet place was on the edge of a lake, she realized a few minutes later when he drew to a stop. The mountain view was all around them. It was a pretty setting, really; a total contrast to the way she was feeling.

It was getting hot. She started to roll down her window, but Drake climbed out of the truck, so she followed.

"It's peaceful out here, isn't it?"

"Is something bothering you, Drake?"

"I'd like to build a house here one day."

Jasmine chuckled. "It's plenty of land for all your stray animals and future children to run wild."

Drake didn't respond.

"I wonder who owns this property."

Drake shrugged.

"Do you feel content, Jasmine?" he asked. "I think you need to resolve your differences with your mother before they leave."

Drake walked over to Jasmine and put his arms around her from behind. "You have a grandfather who loves you. I know things will probably never be good between you, Barbara and Jack, but Steven sees the errors he's made. Your mother loves you. George loves you. Norman loves you, too. Do you think you've finally come to terms with the past?"

"I'm getting there."

"Your mother's human. Yes, she made a few mistakes. But you never told her your problems. Maybe she could have intervened."

"How? She couldn't stay home supervising us

twenty-four-seven. And she certainly wasn't going to leave Norman."

"Maybe you could have had some family communication. Maybe all of you could have seen a counselor. There were options."

"It doesn't matter anymore. It's all in the past."

"Not if it's still front and center in your mind. You need to talk with your mother so you can resolve the past and go on with your life. You need to tell her why you need George in your life."

"I can't tell her. It would hurt her too much."

"You don't have to tell her everything. But she needs to understand what you're feeling."

"I think I've tried to protect her my whole life."

"You don't need to protect her. She's strong." Drake turned her around in his arms, but he didn't kiss her. He merely held her.

"What about you, Drake?" she said against his chest.

Puzzled, he said, "I don't understand."

Jasmine was comforted by the steady beat of Drake's heart. He'd mentioned all the people who loved her. But she noticed he didn't mention himself.

Her arms tightened around his back. She was a fool. She'd fallen in love with him. He'd already told her there wasn't a future for them.

"I've said this many times and you won't respond. I know you're keeping secrets. You refuse to talk to me about it."

Drake eased his hold on her and they moved apart. "Let's talk about it when your family leaves."

"Why are you doing this? I'll only worry."

"Nothing for you to worry about." But the creases between his brows told a different story.

"Is it that bad, Drake?"

"No. It's just something that's been worrying me."

"Are you sick?"

He shook his head. "Nothing like that. Just enjoy your family. We'll talk when they leave." He glanced at his watch. "They must be worrying about you. The way I hauled you out of there."

"That's it? You're going to leave me hanging like that?"

Drake opened his mouth to say something to ease her mind. Maybe tell her he loved her, but what good would that do? All they had was right now. There was no future for them, but he wouldn't tell her that. He'd already gotten himself in too deep. He felt like a louse.

"Let's go," he said.

She stared at him, then tore her gaze away and marched to the truck.

More than anger she felt heartache and betrayal. He was pulling away from her. He wanted to wait until her family left before he ended the relationship.

A few minutes later Drake pulled into her driveway.

"If you want to end the relationship, why don't you just do it right now," she said. "You don't have to wait."

"Stop trying to speculate. We'll talk when your family leaves."

"I mean it, Drake. Don't treat me like a child. I want to know, and now. All I can do is speculate with your being so cryptic. What is it?"

"I can't give you children, Jasmine. I'm physically unable to."

Jasmine stared at him in shock. "Why didn't you tell me?"

"I found out after you arrived. It was hard for *me* to believe. I couldn't even imagine telling you."

Jasmine touched his arm. "Drake, I love you."

"I know. But it's not going to work."

"It can."

"I didn't want to get into this while your family is still here. We'll talk when they leave." He didn't give her a chance to respond and quickly got out of the truck.

Jasmine got out, too, and approached him. "We can't leave something this important..."

"I won't talk about it now." He sighed. "Look, your family is here. You have enough to deal with without my problems."

"I'm not a child, Drake. We're not going to put this on the back burner for later. We're a couple and I think it's important we talk about things." She'd never seen this side of him. He was hurting, and she couldn't let him leave thinking that she would desert him. But he left her side, went into the house to say goodbye to her parents, then he left.

If he could be nurturing to other people, why couldn't he accept it from her? Jasmine sighed when she remembered that she'd already told him she wouldn't adopt or have children from a sperm donor. She had to make this right. So much had happened since she'd arrived in Virginia. She'd been so wrong. She and Drake needed to talk, but they also needed some uninterrupted time.

Later that evening Jasmine approached her mother.

"Mama, Mr. Avery wants us to attend a barbecue at his place Saturday afternoon. Noelle's parents will be there," Jasmine said.

"You know how I feel about associating with that family."

"It's not *that* family. They're half of me."

"Girl, what are you talking about? You are my child." Her mother's lips trembled as she hit herself in the chest. "*My* child."

Right then and there, Jasmine knew she'd never get through to her mother. And she wasn't up to another confrontation.

"You were a dream come true for me. I thought…I thought I'd never have children and I wanted a child so badly. But as much as your father and I tried, we just couldn't. Then we started going through all those tests only to find out your father couldn't have any." She smoothed a hand through Jasmine's hair. "Then a friend told me about the sperm-donor program. I didn't think it would work, but I was desperate. Often it takes months for pregnancy to occur. I was lucky. And then I had you. I can't express the joy you brought into my life. But after your father and I divorced and I remarried, our relationship almost shattered.

"I wanted to do things with you as you grew older, the way we did before I remarried. But you pulled away. I thought it was just teenage rebellion. And you never were one to talk much. I'd talk a mile a minute, but pulling emotions out of you was always difficult."

"It's just…" Jasmine took her mother's hand in hers. "Let's sit." When they were both seated, she continued.

"When I was young, it always felt like a piece of me was missing. And it all came together in my mind when I discovered Dad wasn't my biological father. I looked at my stepbrothers and sister. Their father was always a part of their lives, because he was their father. I didn't understand why Daddy always froze me out. Even with divorce, other fathers participated in their children's lives, at least some of the time. And then Daddy remarried and had another child."

"That wasn't his child," her mother scoffed. "That woman had a baby by another man and passed it off as his, and he was fool enough to believe her lies. Desperate people can make themselves believe anything."

"But he still accepted her. He treated her differently from the way he treated me. And I didn't understand why. I took the bus to their place one day and saw him playing and cuddling with his little girl."

"What?"

"He didn't see me. But the point is, I always thought there was something wrong with me. Something missing, until I found out I was the product of a sperm donor. Half of me was missing. Half of who I was."

"Honey, I loved you from the very beginning."

"I know that. And I know all fathers aren't the way mine was. Noelle's father loves her. He spoils her. He's everything a person could want in a father. Yet she still needed to meet her donor family."

Her mother gazed at her with a sad expression. "I don't know what to say."

"It's like everything is centered around you, the woman who desperately wants a baby. You didn't adopt. The biological significance is so strong that you didn't want to adopt. You wanted your own. Why can't you understand that my biological history is just as important to me? You won't lose me. You're still my mom. Nothing will ever change that."

Amanda looked as if she'd run smack into a brick wall and tethered there waiting to fall flat on her face.

Maybe Jasmine had said too much. Maybe this talk hadn't been a good idea after all. What the heck did Drake know?

Amanda cleared her throat. "It…It's that important that I see this man?"

"He's my grandfather. He's the first man who ever wanted me, just because I'm me. Other than Drake, that is. Can you imagine how that feels, Mama?"

Amanda's eyes were sad when they gazed into her daughter's soul. "Okay," she said quietly. "I'll have dinner at River Oaks."

"Thanks, Mama."

Her mother stood. "Now, let's get ready to tour some of those little shops you've been raving about."

Jasmine knew her mother's brisk manner covered a world of hurt. She didn't know how to breach it. Perhaps with time, they'd both find the closeness they were searching for. Hadn't they made progress so far? Far more than she'd expected this trip.

Telling Jasmine of his sterility had been very difficult for Drake. How did you tell a woman you're everything she *doesn't* want in a man? He wasn't ready for it to be over, but he couldn't force her to do something she was totally against.

Drake sighed tiredly. Hugs nuzzled up to him and he scratched behind the dog's ears, then found a biscuit for her and tossed it. Hugs went scampering across the floor to fetch it. That would keep her busy for a few minutes.

Steven came in with a towel over his shoulder. "What're we going to do tonight?"

"Whatever you want." The truth was, Drake didn't want to do a thing but keep his own company. But Colin had invited them over to play cards. It was Friday night and his brothers were coming to the farm. Maybe a game would keep his mind off his misery. He told Steven about the game.

"Sounds good to me. I usually win."

Jasmine didn't see Drake again until the barbecue. He looked as bad as she felt. They were both suffering for no reason. She loved him.

She and Drake stayed out of each other's way. And although her mother had been friendly on the surface, Jasmine knew she didn't totally accept Mr. Avery. Though, Lord knows, he tried with all his enormous charm. Charm just didn't work with her mother. Jasmine couldn't complain, though. All in all, the barbecue had gone better than expected.

Sunday arrived very quickly. Although they had driven a rental car, Norman turned it in while Jasmine drove to the airport with her mother. Jasmine parked her car in the short-term parking so she could spend a few minutes more with her mother before she left.

Her mother went to the ticket counter to check in. Then she joined Jasmine.

"I'm so glad I came."

"So am I," Jasmine said.

"I couldn't help but notice there seemed to be a problem with you and Drake."

"We'll sort it out, Mom. Don't worry about it."

"I always worry, whether you tell me to or not." They walked toward the security checkpoint. "This week feels like a month has passed instead of merely a week."

A lot of milestones had taken place. "I know."

"Come visit me. Your siblings won't be there."

"I will, Mama. As soon as I can get a vacation. I hope Jack and Barbara make the plane."

"If they don't, they're grown. They can get themselves back to L.A."

"I can't believe my mother is talking this way."

"I've done my duty. Stay safe, sweetheart."

"Love you, Mom." After they hugged, her mother went through the security screening, picked up her purse and waved back at Jasmine.

Jasmine started to head home, but it was time to deal with Drake—and their future.

* * *

When Jasmine made it to Drake's house, his truck was in the yard, but he didn't answer the door.

She went around to the back of the house. He was sitting on the deck, nursing a glass of wine.

"Drake…"

There was a mixture of dread and hope in his eyes. Hugs rose from her sitting position to meet Jasmine. She played with the dog for a bit while she gathered her thoughts.

"Did your family get off okay?" Drake asked. He swallowed the rest of the wine as if he needed fortification and tipped his chin. "I love you, Jasmine, but I can't marry you." He cleared his throat. "I can't even propose to you. The woman I marry will either have to have children already or, if she wants them, she'd have to go through the same kind of donor program your mother went through. I know how she must have felt. But I won't ask you to do that because you're so against it."

Stunned, Jasmine came the rest of the way up the stairs. She felt as if a bomb had landed on her and she needed to know how to go to get out of the wreckage. But he'd said he loved her. He couldn't ask her to marry him because he couldn't have children.

So he wanted to marry her.

"Why didn't you tell me this from the beginning?"

He sighed, rubbing the back of his neck. For the first time they broke eye contact. "I didn't know how."

"And you didn't think our relationship would have ever gotten off the ground?"

He didn't respond.

Could it be he was afraid of losing her? It was true, she had been so bitter when she arrived that she might have never given them a chance. But, he'd done so much since she got into town. He had really been her ship in the storm. Was she willing to give that up? Especially since he loved her. Love didn't come easily. Not for her. If nothing else, there was one truth she could give him.

She reached across the abyss and grabbed his hand. His hand tightened in hers as if he were trying to hold back all kinds of emotions.

"I love you, Drake. We can make this work."

"How? I want children." He raised his hand and let it drop. "You want children."

"Well, we can go the donor route."

He was shaking his head before the words emerged.

"Don't you see? It wasn't the program and it wasn't my mother or Mackenzie. It was my father's attitude. I can see that now. I was painting the entire program with the same brush."

He looked as if he was afraid to believe that she really was accepting the situation.

"Hey, I'm the cautious one," Jasmine said. "What happened to the guy who's always willing to go headfirst?"

Drake chuckled. But he still gazed at her as if he couldn't believe what he was hearing.

"You know, the hardest part is finding love, and the one thing I know about you is your enormous capacity to love." She caressed his cheek. "If you can love those misfit animals enough to spend your hard-earned cash on them, you can love any child we have. I trust you, Drake."

Drake cleared his throat. "I can't…"

"Besides, who knows what'll happen in the future? This sperm thing is changing all the time."

"We can't count on that, Jasmine."

"I can count on you and your love."

"And that's enough?"

Jasmine smiled. "It's more than enough."

Drake's heart expanded and contracted. He'd never believed this could happen to him. He pulled

Jasmine onto his lap so fast she screamed and then laughed in delight. Hugs bounded over to them to join in the fun.

His life couldn't get more perfect than it was at that moment.

From boardroom to bedroom...

Brenda JACKSON

In Bed with Her Boss

Though D'marcus Armstrong is a demanding, cranky
boss, he's the star of Opal Lockhart's fantasies. But
what chance does a buttoned-up, naive secretary have
with this self-made millionaire? A pretty good one
actually...when Opal's sisters come to the rescue
with a makeover and some attitude adjustment!

THE LOCKHARTS
THREE WEDDINGS & A REUNION

*Available the first week of August
wherever books are sold.*

KIMANI™
ROMANCE

www.kimanipress.com

KPBJ0280807

Wanted: Good Christian woman

ESSENCE BESTSELLING AUTHOR

Jacquelin Thomas

The Pastor's Woman

New preacher Wade Kendrick wants a reserved, traditional woman for a wife—but he only has eyes for Pearl Lockhart, aka Ms. Wrong. Pearl aspires to gospel stardom and doesn't fit into the preacher's world. But their sexual chemistry downright sizzles. What's a sister to do?

THE LOCKHARTS

THREE WEDDINGS AND A REUNION

FOR FOUR SASSY SISTERS, ROMANCE CHANGES EVERYTHING!

Available the first week of September wherever books are sold.

KIMANI™
ROMANCE

The follow-up to *Sweet Surrender*
and *Here and Now...*

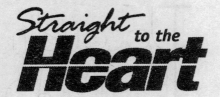

Straight to the
Heart

Bestselling author

MICHELLE MONKOU

Fearful that her unsavory past is about to be exposed,
hip-hop diva Stacy Watts dates clean-cut Omar Masterson
to save her new image. But their playacting backfires
when their mutual attraction starts to burn out of control!
Now Stacy must fight to keep the secrets of her past
from destroying her future with Omar.

*Available the first week of September
wherever books are sold.*

KIMANI™
ROMANCE

www.kimanipress.com   KPMM0340907

He was the first man to touch her soul...

SOUL
Caress

Favorite author

KIMSHAW

When privileged Kennedy Daniels loses her sight,
hospital orderly Malik Crawford helps heal her
wounds and awaken her desire. But they come from
different worlds, so unless Kennedy's willing to defy her
prominent family, a future between them is impossible.

*Available the first week of September
wherever books are sold.*

KIMANI
ROMANCE™

www.kimanipress.com   KPKS0350907

Essence bestselling author

DONNA

Hill

She's ready for her close-up...

Moments Like This

Part of the Romance in the Spotlight series

Actress and model Dominique Laws has been living the
Hollywood dream—fame, fortune, a handsome husband—
but lately good roles have been scarce. Then she learns
that her business-manager husband has been cheating
on her personally and financially. Suddenly, she's down
and out in Beverly Hills. But a chance meeting with a
Denzel-fine filmmaker may offer the role of a lifetime....

**Available the first week of September,
wherever books are sold.**

ARABESQUE®

www.kimanipress.com   KPDH0190907